Death and a Madonna

By Joan O'Hagan

DEATH AND A MADONNA
INCLINE AND FALL

Death and a Madonna

JOAN O'HAGAN

PUBLISHED FOR THE CRIME CLUB BY
DOUBLEDAY & COMPANY, INC.
GARDEN CITY, NEW YORK
1987

All of the characters in this book
are fictitious, and any resemblance
to actual persons, living or dead,
is purely coincidental.

Library of Congress Cataloging-in-Publication Data
O'Hagan, Joan.
Death and a Madonna.
I. Title.
PR9619.3.038D4   1987   823   87-5347
ISBN 0-385-24306-5

For Denise and Jim

Death and a Madonna

Prologue

Of course, the telephone would ring just at that point, shattering the stillness and sending his thoughts to the winds. And, when he rushed to answer it, a contained silence, a click as the receiver went down at the other end. A dead line.

The second time in an hour. Charles Mowbray, art historian, walked slowly back to his desk. No peace—not even here in his apartment tucked away in that impregnable fortress, the Palazzo Doria, in the centre of old Rome. He took up his pen and settled his glasses on his nose, bending his strong and handsome face to his notes. But he had lost the thread now. What a waste of inspiration; and yet, his latest book—on the art of the Baroque this time—would be very good. A landmark in its way. If it only sold . . .

In the harsh rays of a reading lamp, he was suddenly an old man, with a slack throat and sagging cheeks, the corners of the mouth pointing downwards. He got up again and made for the dining room. Darkness there. Raffaella could not be in yet, he didn't know why. Only back a few days after leaving him to fend for himself, while she took leave from her office to go abroad. A devil of a time he had had of it too, left to the casual ministrations of the new maid, Elena. A sly-looking woman. Italian name, Crispoldi, but came from Tripoli or somewhere. She spoke English and French besides Italian, admittedly, and so was more useful than the usual kind of maid. But he didn't like her and somehow didn't trust her either. And the money they had to pay her. Wages plus insurance, plus bus fares, plus holiday money, plus this monstrous thirteenth month the Italians added to their working year.

Dr. Mowbray poured himself a Scotch. At least he got that cheap, as Raffaella was allowed to use the Consortium's commissary. He went back to his study and, drawing aside a curtain of a rich plum red on the wall facing his desk, uncovered a Madonna dreaming over the Child. Against a dark background, her skin gleamed with the subtle flesh tones given by the great Venetian master who had painted her; and her sad, wise gaze seemed once more to Dr. Mowbray to breathe the very essence of the religious devotion of that long-gone century. He sat down at his desk and fell into a reverie, and it was thus, some twenty minutes later, that his wife found him as she entered, laden with parcels.

"Ah, there you are at last. I'm most damnably hungry, m'dear." His tone was somewhat plaintive. "What on earth kept you?" He looked, as always, with pleasure on her tall and rather full figure, a true Italian figure of the old style, rather big in the hips, just a shade thick in the legs, but dignified and well set up. Shouldn't wear slacks, though, silly girl, as she often did.

"The traffic was impossible." Her face was strained.

"See you're not late tomorrow night, Raffaella. I'm anxious to begin on time."

"Oh!" She started, and set down her parcels. "I meant to tell you . . ." She was keeping her eyes from his. "I can't do the lectures."

"Eh? You mean you won't look after the projector?"

"Please . . . I'd rather not."

"But you've always done it. We even arranged the lectures at the highly inconvenient hour of five-forty-five to accommodate you. And afterwards I'd like to offer them a drink or something."

"Leaving the office on time will be very difficult for the next few weeks. We are very busy."

"Oh rubbish! You've always been able to twist old what's-his-name round your finger and you agreed to do this simply ages ago. It quite spoils the whole thing if I have to fool round holding books and pictures on the epidiascope and turn lamps on and off continuously . . ."

"Perhaps one of the class—"

"They don't pay their not inconsiderable money in advance to fuss round with slides. Anyway, you've done it so often now that you're quite efficient at it."

"All right, Charles." She shrugged, suddenly surrendering.

"That's a good girl now. Remember, we'll net more than four million lire with this course. I rely on you not to slip me up . . ."

Oh God, he moaned inwardly. Raffaella! Why can't I talk to you now? Why do I have to go on in this pedagogical fashion—half-jocular, half-carping? Why can I never *say anything* I want to you nowadays?

She was—uncharacteristically—flushing now.

"Four million lire, in return for the work and inconvenience, and the apartment filled with these stupid, rich women, gaping and seeing . . . seeing . . . Never before have you had to descend to this kind of thing!"

"Come now, Raffaella! How you exaggerate."

"Oh, *do* I!" She snatched a list of names from his desk. "Look at them—Consortium wives. In the morning," she hooted ironically, "they will read two pages of *I Promessi Sposi*—and thus they deal with Italian literature. In the afternoon they listen to you, or pretend to, and learn some painters' names. And then they know Italian art." Her voice cut like a knife. "Mrs. Doris Boot. Mme. Juliette Deneuve. Mrs. Hedda Hardegen. Mrs. Beverley *Backhouse* . . ."

But here Raffaella choked.

"Oh come, Raffaella." Mowbray stared hard at her. "Juliette Deneuve isn't Consortium, and she paints herself. I saw something of hers once—now where was it? It had something. Are you being quite fair?"

Raffaella returned his stare stormily. Then abruptly she shrugged and fled from the study. Mowbray heard the click of the telephone as she dialled. He sighed. Like all Italians, her daily life seemed to hang on long telephone calls, about what God only knew.

Then immediately after dinner, she told him she had to go out. She did not ask if he minded, but simply rushed off. How she had changed lately. Far less attentive to his wants. Five years ago, when he had married her, how fond she had been of him, his beautiful, talkative girl. *Dulce ridentem Lalagen amabo, dulce loquentem* . . . The words came instinctively to his mind, as she talked away so charmingly, so intelligently. How he had loved to watch her, her creamy neck rising from her shoulders with the grace and dignity of a Piero della Francesca model. Never would he forget his first sight of her—or sound. How delightfully had her laughter, so spontaneous and fresh, bubbled forth from those well-shaped lips of hers. But nowadays she did not chatter much, if she was there at all, and hardly ever did she laugh.

Backdrop

I

Beverley Backhouse. Hedda Hardegen . . .

But Raffaella Mowbray hadn't been fair to *them*, because both knew—and loved—Rome, in all its moods. And though foreign, either might have leapt to life under the brush of some Renaissance painter. Locked together, this cold, threatening February morning, in a world of their own, their long slender jeans-clad legs straddling a big Japanese motor cycle, weaving skilfully through the traffic on the Lungotevere Sangallo. Each with a delicate subtlety of line and colouring that belonged to Florence rather than Rome. Hedda, in control of the cycle, with the pale smooth profile of a girl by Botticelli, while Beverley, with her shining chestnut hair, had escaped from some cloud-borne painted troop of angels.

Beverley, arms wound tightly about Hedda's waist, watched great sculptured storm-clouds massing over Roman domes and roof-tops and the gleam of golden travertine. As the Ponte Sant'Angelo rushed at them, Bernini's marble angels, poised on the parapet, soared briefly above and were gone in a flash. There came a surge of power as Hedda accelerated—and wild elation, a surrender to speed, to the rush of dry air, to ear-splitting noise.

They were headed for an art show, to which they had been invited by formal invitation, and they were much behind schedule. Naturally, because in Rome no one is ever on time.

No, Raffaella shouldn't have lumped them in with the other Consortium wives. But Mowbray could not have known—as Raffaella didn't tell him—how, in the crush of the Via del

Babuino that morning, she had seen the two of them. They had chained their big Mitsuzuki to a post and come towards her, close together, swaggering just a little in their high-heeled leather boots.

Then Beverley, catching sight of Raffaella, suddenly changed into the wife of John Backhouse, high official of the Anglo-European Banking Consortium. Regal even.

"Raffaella Mowbray, Hedda. *You* know, John's secretary."

Tinkling away, patronising Raffaella . . .

"A friend has some stuff in this art show. Juliette Deneuve. I'm sure *you* know all about painting, don't you, Raffaella? Hedda, you know Raffaella's husband is Dr. Charles Mowbray—the man who is to lecture us on Italian art . . ."

And Raffaella had been dragged into the Galleria Gianicolo, crammed with bodies, ringing like an orchestra pit with the discord of three score Italian voices tuning up for full performance. John Backhouse's wife had forced her in here, but Raffaella wasn't going to form part of Juliette Deneuve's claque. So, after looking at half a dozen Deneuve landscapes, Raffaella had gestured languidly.

"This picture lacks balance. Lacks a centre. This *casotto,* so badly placed, this clump of trees, put here without artistic reason. It hesitates, this painting . . ."

And with the first rush of words, suddenly defining her position. Secure now, cool and even insolent.

She'd gone on talking, then.

"Questi dilettanti." Raising her voice against the din. "It is the way of art today. All paint, because it is the fashion . . ."

Then, crazily, out of the blue, a voice behind her breathing her name, a voice she would have known anywhere, and had thought never to hear again—

"Raffaella!"

Swinging round, to look into the grey-blue eyes rarely seen in Italians, such a contrast to the olive skin and the luxurious black waves of his hair. Renato Barbicinti. She'd been struck dumb; while, after the first shock, Renato, aware that all heads had turned and the orchestra about them was lulled, expectantly, obeying the mysterious pianissimo of an unseen conductor, had said lightly:

"Che bella sorpresa!" and had drawn her aside, talking easy nothings, while his eyes, searching her face, told her much else. "I was offered this gallery and, on an impulse—here I am. Why not? I've been out of the country a long time, and Milano, after San Paolo, especially in midwinter . . ."

Renato, here in the Via del Babuino, managing a gallery.

Raffaella had turned back to find an American couple confronting her. The man was talking and her eyes had travelled up an impeccable shirt-front to a rugged face all amused deprecation.

"My wife had taken a great fancy to this painting. But you were saying it is badly arranged, Ma'am."

"Design is not everything." Raffaella spoke absently now, hardly aware of what she was saying. "I do not care for it, it is all." Her eyes swung to Beverley, standing by the American. Colour tinged her polished cheeks. Her shrug damned the painting to eternity.

The man and his wife had been talking, then, but she hadn't heard a word. And then, from behind a row of canvases, a statuesque figure had emerged dramatically, a woman with auburn hair and brown eyes. She seemed to be throwing off the restraining hands of unseen attendants. Pausing, as the American had pursed his lips judiciously and turned to his wife. "Almost a thousand dollars . . . You don't want trees in the wrong place for that money." Had he been joking? At any rate, he and his wife had bowed and disappeared in the crush. And the symphony swelled to crescendo.

The auburn-haired woman had addressed Beverley and Hedda, her nervous fingers plucking at them. But her eyes attacked Raffaella.

"What a pleasure to see you here, Beverley! And you, Hedda!" The strongly accented words tumbling out on a breathless rush of emotion. Then, turning to Raffaella, coaxing and insidious. "You have criticised the colour of this painting, Madame. Do tell me more . . ."

Raffaella had stared haughtily at the newcomer, and pronounced the colour "immature."

"All dabs and blobs and streaks," she shrugged. "How gaudy.

And it produces nothing. Only a very good artist knows to dab like that."

"Cara Signora!" Barbicinti insinuated himself skilfully between the two women. "For every painting there are one hundred and more appreciations of it, *non è vero?"*

But the Frenchwoman's words had issued in an insurmountable torrent. "I thank you, Madame, for exposing the defects . . . and with such facility . . ."

Furious, she had retreated, led by the gallery manager, into a back room. Raffaella had left the gallery immediately.

After Raffaella had gone, Beverley heard a man behind her say:

"Excuse me. Was that Juliette Deneuve?"

Beverley turned to face a stocky flaxen-haired man of perhaps thirty-five. A fleshy but good-looking face, a hard mouth. He put his head close to hers, speaking against the renewed volume of the background chorus.

Beverley nodded.

"She did all the paintings along this side."

"I don't share the Italian lady's opinion, then," he returned. "They are the best things in this exhibition. Look at number thirty-five . . ."

"Yes, it's first class."

"It breathes the *Campagna* on a spring morning."

"You know Rome, then?" Beverley looked at his skin, red from suns other than the thin Roman sun of winter. He nodded and smiled, his light-blue eyes glistening, boring rudely into her face. "I do a lot of travelling." His voice was a smooth baritone, and in it two accents fought.

On an impulse Beverley asked:

"Do you come from Australia?"

He said, a little patronisingly, "You've got a sharp ear."

"Officially, I'm Australian myself. But you only say *some* words like an Australian."

"And you, no words!" He bowed mockingly and took a card from his breast pocket. His jacket seemed barely to contain the burly body beneath.

The card gave an address in Sydney, and informed her that

Mr. André Van Dam was representing the Barrington Lett Galleries, with headquarters in Martin Place.

"I'm on the prowl, as they say," Van Dam said simply. "For painting talent," he added with a smile. But his bold blue eyes were saying that he found her desirable.

Together they finished viewing, Hedda following in their wake with an aloof expression. When they were through, Van Dam said: "We might have a drink or something and compare notes on Rome."

Hedda burst into the conversation, unceremoniously and definitely.

"We can't." She pressed Beverley's arm warningly.

"No, we can't really," echoed Beverley uncertainly.

Van Dam produced another card and said:

"I'd like to have a word with Juliette Deneuve."

"Juliette's very upset. I'll go and tell her you want to see her."

"Then we've got to go," Hedda insisted.

"Yes." Beverley's voice trembled between laughter and sorrow. "Then we've got to go."

They found Juliette seated, half reclining, on a velvet couch in Barbicinti's office, while he held her hand. Juliette sipped cognac. The young Italian looked relieved at their appearance.

"When two ladies disagree . . ." He waved an expressive hand and smiled with pleasure. *"Niente da fare.* A pity. Both so beautiful. I am more than grieved that it should have happened." His good-looking face, across which there sped a look of fatuous regret, could not have settled more quickly into lines of unconcern.

"In one short morning," Juliette breathed, sipping the cognac with which he had just replenished her glass, "my confidence as an artist, even as a woman, is destroyed."

"Oh Juliette, you're not serious!"

"The first brutal blow to my pride and my art." Juliette's lips trembled. "And the man, the American, he was buying it, he was buying it. And then she come along." On her second glass, her English was suffering. A tear spilled out of each brown eye.

"Cheer up. Another man out there wants to see you. He's crazy about your paintings."

Juliette quivered and said tremulously: "He wants to see me?"

She took the card which Beverley held out and they watched elation banish grief from her countenance, in touchingly fast stages.

"You should certainly see him," said Barbicinti, peering over Juliette's shoulder. "It could mean business."

"Yes, yes." Juliette rose majestically and snatched her hand-bag, from which issued a medley of comb, paint and powder. "First I will complete myself . . ."

They left her, courting the mirror.

"I'm hungry," said Beverley, outside in the street.

"What a *poseuse* Juliette is." Hedda wrinkled her nose disdainfully.

"Artistic. I think she's rather vulnerable underneath. Of course, Raffaella was *awful*. Absolutely scathing. I don't know why . . ."

Hedda looked at her ironically.

"Probably Raffaella lumps Juliette in with most Consortium wives—useless, rich, overbearing bitches, who like to think they know all about art and all that."

"But Juliette isn't a Consortium wife."

Hedda shrugged.

"You are. Maybe she just wanted to take *you* down, indirectly. The boss's wife."

Over lunch, Hedda launched her own attack.

"Why *did* you drag the Mowbray woman along, anyway?"

"Why shouldn't I?"

"You can't miss a chance to make me squirm, can you?" Hedda's voice was suddenly fierce.

"I don't . . . I didn't . . . I just was so happy, Heddy. Can't you see I was just so happy?" Suddenly Beverley's voice was choked with tears.

"Two half-portions of lasagne, ladies," hissed the waiter, banging down the plates carelessly in front of them and splashing wine into their glasses. "You want also de mineral water?"

Hedda shifted her eyes from Beverley's face and scowled at him:

"Half a litre."

"Don't be crazy, Heddy." Beverley attempted a melting smile.

"Does the Mowbray visit your house?"

"Eh? Once or twice, ages ago. Why shouldn't she?"

Hedda said deliberately:

"If you all three of you get some perverted kick out of it—you and John and her—I guess it's O.K."

Beverley set down her fork, staring at Hedda.

"All three . . . but you don't mean her and *John!* Oh Heddy." She spun the words out incredulously.

Hedda became motionless.

"You didn't *know!* When the whole Consortium knows. And for God knows how long!"

Beverley sat transfixed for a long moment, thinking carefully, going back over months, years. Then her chin went up proudly. "Well, well." She laughed suddenly, a little tinkling laugh. "My husband is nearly fifty, Hed."

"Remember old Bellows at school?"

Beverley laughed again, weakly this time.

"It's true, isn't it, wives are the last to find out. What now, I wonder?" Her voice dragged.

"You don't mean to say you *care!*" Hedda burst out.

Beverley was silent.

"You told me," stammered Hedda, "you don't sleep with him. You haven't for ages."

Beverley sat as though turned to marble.

"You don't . . . you aren't in *love* with him!" Hedda was white in the face, rigid.

Beverley shook her head distractedly. What was love? She didn't know. She wanted Hedda. But moments ago, John had struck her to the heart.

"You've told me you don't care—lots of times," Hedda was panicking now.

Beverley's eyes dropped before hers.

"You just have to have everyone . . . everyone your slave—bowing and scraping. *Don't* you!" Hedda's eyes burned.

"No."

"Yes. Like at school. You just can't resist playing people along."

"All right then!" Beverley said wildly. "I'll show you. I'll leave John."

"What crazy idea have you got in your head now?"

"I'll leave him. I'll leave Rome."

"You *won't.*"

"Oh, won't I? I'll leave Rome and I'll find a job some place. London, maybe."

"Don't talk rubbish," said Hedda scornfully. "You can't *do* anything. You're not trained for anything. *You*'ve only had an expensive education."

Beverley was silent, looking at her sullenly now.

"You can't leave *me*, you little fool. It'd be *terrible.*" Hedda gripped the edge of the table.

The waiter came up. Hedda looked up and through him and said: "We're going now. Bring the bill."

"Don't be silly," Beverley protested. She was stung to anger. "We haven't had the steak."

The waiter raised his eyes to heaven.

"We'll have the steak," said Beverley.

When it came she ate fiercely through it, talking brightly, on the verge of tears.

Hedda, remorseful now, slid a hand across the table and fondled the fist clenched around Beverley's wineglass.

Afterwards, winding with muted spluttering roar through narrow back-streets towards the Piazza Venezia, Hedda said abruptly to the head resting in the hollow of her shoulder:

"What if I got Raffaella Mowbray dismissed from the Consortium? Rudolf was talking about staff reductions the other night."

"Sent away from the Consortium?"

"Do you want it?"

Beverley didn't answer, but the added pressure of her arms said yes.

II

By soon after five-thirty the following evening, the air in Mowbray's reception room was alive with the aborted, slightly hysterical chirruping of the ladies attending the first of the doctor's lectures on Italian painting. They were grouped naturally around Lady Loftus, tall and plain, slightly anxious of face, wife of the director of the Anglo-European Banking Consortium.

"A walk through the *Medioevo* to get here," she was proclaiming. "Like a dungeon these long stone corridors, three-foot walls and iron bars. The inhabitants are safe from thieves in the Palazzo Doria." She glanced round at the ladies and against renewed chattering added: "Mrs. Boot is still to come."

"Who is Mrs. Boot?" asked a goodhumoured-looking American woman.

"Husband is our new head of Operational Research and Systems Analysis," said Lady Loftus briefly.

Juliette Deneuve alone disdained forming part of Lady Loftus's entourage and moved, with absorbed attention, from one *objet d'art* to another—for Mowbray's reception room was richly decorated—while she exclaimed softly to herself.

"I never knew the Mowbrays lived in such a wonderful old palazzo as this!" Beverley, her head held high, came in with Hedda.

"I hear things about your husband," said Lady Loftus quietly, putting her arm round Beverley's shoulder and drawing her aside. "My *dear!* What *is* it?" Beverley had started violently.

"Oh nothing . . ."

"I mean his promotion to head up LETDEB. Splendid news. I was so fearful a certain other person might get it."

"Thank you, Lady Loftus. Very kind of you."

"There is really no one else I should have preferred to see charged with that responsibility," pronounced Lady Loftus. "We're likely to see a little more of each other from now on as a result, of course, which I'm not at all averse to, really not at all. And William feels the same."

"Thank you, Lady Loftus . . ."

"By the way, I think you might call me 'Mary' from now on," added the lady blandly.

Meeting Hedda's eye, Beverley giggled uncontrollably.

"There's your Mrs. Boot now, I should think," said the American woman bluntly. "Hello," she said breezily, going up to a small, dark, brightly dressed woman who had just appeared at the door. "Come along in. I guess you're the missing Boot."

"Welcome." Lady Loftus sailed forward and Jo Ann Partridge found herself suddenly in the wings, though she had not moved position, while Lady Loftus had the centre of the stage. "Welcome to the group. Come, everyone, and meet Mrs. Boot."

Names were thrown back and forth for a moment or so, and then the buzz died down suddenly with the entrance, from the other side of the room, of Dr. Mowbray, a tall, impressive figure with his silver hair, fine dark eyes and handsome, haughty face. Raffaella followed and immediately disappeared behind a Chinese screen, so placed as to hide the projector and all its works.

"You know a great deal about art in Italy, all of you," Dr. Mowbray began, without ceremony. "You know even more than you think you know. It's inevitable. You can't go about this city, travel through the Italian countryside, without being confronted continuously by the greatest feast of artistic outpouring that the world has ever seen. Even Nature partakes of it.

"These, then, will not be lectures in the ordinary sense of the word, but a grouping, an arrangement, a drawing together of threads, a filling in of the background to your own already considerable artistic knowledge and intelligent study."

A little ripple of gratification ran through his audience.

"I have it in mind to begin with a brief account of the artist— that is, the painter, sculptor and architect—over the centuries, commencing with the ancient world of Greece and Rome. We will then turn to Florentine painting in particular, and then to that of Venice."

They gave themselves up to the lecture. As well they might. It was beautifully delivered, expertly illustrated, drew—after well over an hour—to a climax, and almost thundered to a close. Hardly used to such brilliance, they relaxed by stages, found their tongues, and made gladly for the tray of drinks which the maid handed round. Extravagant compliments were thrown at Dr. Mowbray, who smiled his thanks and retired to his study for a few moments' respite.

"He is truly a first-class speaker," cried Juliette to Mrs. Boot, next to whom she had ended up. "And like all successful speakers, he acts the part as well, you notice this, no?" she demanded. "So handsome as he is, he might be on the stage, do you not agree?"

Doris Boot stared stolidly at her.

"You might be right at that."

"He lives his lecture," declaimed Juliette. She took a glass from the dark, sharp-eyed woman in maid's uniform who appeared, respectfully murmuring something, at her elbow. But it was obvious that Juliette's attention at that moment was suddenly riveted on some person on the other side of the room. Abruptly she left Doris and went straight over to Dr. Mowbray, who at that moment had appeared in the doorway of his study.

"If I could perhaps speak to you alone," she asked, in her headlong, impulsive fashion. She was greatly agitated, he could see.

"Your lecture—superb!" she breathed. *"C'était d'une qualité merveilleuse, je vous assure.* How much would I adore to continue with this class."

He could only step back into his study before this determined advance, and she followed impetuously. While he closed the door behind them, she looked round with interest.

"Mais c'est magnifique!" Her eyes rested on the Madonna and Child. "Bellini, *n'est-ce pas?* What an artist is this, but truly."

"I'm very happy with this copy," commented Dr. Mowbray. "A very good friend of mine did it."

For some minutes Juliette gazed at the painting in complete silence.

"One would think it original, *vraiment."* She clasped her hands, her eyes shining.

"One really would, it's true," he laughed. "I see you know a lot about painting, Madame."

"I have studied for many years." Juliette made a little gesture. "I paint, perhaps badly."

She coloured, and Mowbray gazed with admiration as she

drew herself up, imagining that big luxuriant body unclothed. She was full of colour, in warm autumn tones, and it was probable that undressed she might be very like a Giulio Romano nymph. Or Rubens? Yes, one of the Three Graces.

"Such artistic appreciation as yours can hardly go with bad painting, my dear lady," he remarked quietly.

She shrugged.

"It is not what I wish to talk of. It is this—that sorry as I am, I do not find it possible to continue with your lectures."

"Oh, what a pity. Is it an inconvenient hour for you?"

"I find . . . I cannot . . . be in the same room as a certain person."

"Oh, really? And may I ask . . . who?"

"The lady who does the photographs," burst out Juliette. "She criticise my paintings, those displayed in the Galleria Gianicolo only since Tuesday. She is most cruel, and speaks so all those present in the gallery may hear. She does me such an injury as never have I suffer in my life previous."

"You can't mean Raffaella, surely!"

"Her name I do not know. She cannot be . . . Oh my God, have I criticised your daughter?"

"If you mean Raffaella," he replied a little stiffly, "she is my wife."

"I say no more," said Juliette excitedly. "I say too much. Sir, I extend my great apologies. And I would only ask, for the sum that I spend, to be refunded."

"Oh, if it's only Raffaella who's troubling you," he exclaimed, "you really shouldn't worry about what *she* says. Lord, she doesn't know about painting, you know. She only thinks she does. Which gallery did you say? The Gianicolo? I must get in and have a look at your things."

"You would do me a great honour." Juliette smiled brilliantly. "*Your* opinion, I accept!"

"But I do hope you'll continue to come to the lectures. Of all the class you will be the only one to whom I can reasonably talk on this level."

"You are persuasive." She smiled again. "I think . . . perhaps I could change my mind in this respect. For the moment, I remain for the next lecture."

Her eyes shining, she withdrew. In the hall, the class prepared volubly for departure. Juliette went straight up to Beverley.

"I have something to tell you," she breathed.

Beverley, caught struggling with her heavy topcoat, dropped her handbag on the marble floor.

"I am clumsy!" Juliette, hastening to pick up the pretty pouch, managed to spill the entire contents to the floor. Lady Loftus, bending to retrieve a lipstick which had rolled to her feet, exclaimed:

"Beverley! What's this? A gun!"

"It's all right." Beverley's eyes mocked her. "Hedda is teaching me."

"Well!"

"After what happened to the Brentanos last month."

"Thieves were waiting for him and his wife when they got home," explained Hedda. "Underneath, in the apartment garage. They bound and gagged his wife and forced him to take them up and open his own flat while they did it over. A real haul. All the silver, furs—the lot."

"I hope you know how to use it, Beverley," said Lady Loftus severely.

"I told you. I'm learning." Beverley moved her body impatiently.

"She's already a dead shot," asserted Hedda, her heavy-lidded eyes impassive.

Doris Boot, waiting for Juliette, who had offered her a lift, put her head close to Jo Ann Partridge and whispered:

"I know they tip a lot in this country, but we surely don't have to tip the maid here."

"First I ever heard of it," said Jo Ann.

"Juliette did," said Doris baldly, her eyes on the Swiss artist.

"Waal, I sure won't follow her example," said Jo Ann tartly. "Er, how much . . ."

"Ah, that I couldn't see," said Doris regretfully.

"Phew!" Mowbray breathed a sigh as he closed the door behind the last of the ladies, and took a letter from the mail-box for his

apartment. "Three hours of 'em. I wonder if I'm getting too old
. . . Raffaella!"

There was no reply. He poured himself a Scotch and settled
in an armchair. Elena the maid had gone, and he could hear the
subdued murmur of Raffaella's voice on the extension telephone in the dining room. She had shut the door however.
Moodily, he opened the unstamped envelope and read the
three typewritten lines on the single sheet of paper inside:

> You may be interested to know that last month your wife
> shared a suite for a week in the Hôtel George V, Paris, with
> Mr. John Backhouse.

Raffaella, pacing her bedroom floor, later reviewed her situation with Latin lack of sentiment. She thought of John Backhouse. Dear John, how different from Charles, with his all-too-
ready and cruel tongue, his lofty, slightly patronising attitude to
her own opinions on things artistic, his impatience with ignorance, so remote in his cocoon of specialist knowledge. Didn't
his paintings mean more to him, in the long run, than people of
flesh and blood? How condescendingly he had looked on her
own early efforts to paint. And always so immersed in his reading, in his lectures, in research for his interminable books.

She had supposed that her job would come to an end on
marriage to so eminent a man. But somehow the time was
never opportune. And now—Raffaella's eyes grew very dark—
things would never change, as long as she stayed with Charles.
He would get older and older, and she would continue working,
until finally she was old too—old and worn out. Lack of money
would dog her days to the end.

John, on the other hand, John—on the surface so massively,
ponderously almost, the investment banker, the man of affairs,
concerned with weighty matters, with his horn-rims and judi-
cial air—was inside a man of powerful emotions. Raffaella's fine
lips curled. She felt she had discovered him, almost created
him, that inner man. Of one thing she was certain: he was
entirely in her power. For all his business acumen and professional sophistication, the man beneath had an amazing capacity
to treat a woman reverently, almost humbly. And he had re-

spect for her intellect. Five years she had worked for him, and always he had staunchly protected her, cherished her.

With John, she would have the status and money she had never had with Charles. Money brought freedom and leisure, two very valuable commodities. And although not all important, the apartment which Raffaella had in mind for herself and John on the Aventine Hill, looking out towards the Palatine across the Circo Massimo, which was to be sold in six months' time, would be delightful. What holidays they would have, the world over . . .

With such pleasant thoughts to entertain her, the wonder was that she felt so unhappy.

III

"What, then, constitutes a work of art?" demanded Dr. Mowbray, preparing to wind up a lecture. He raised his handsome head and looked round challengingly.

"We might say," he continued, "with the traditionalists, that a work of art constitutes an object of beauty. It is a work to please the eyes, stir the emotions, excite the intellect, rouse passion and delight—and feed the spirit. And yet, we would hardly call a host of modern works beautiful. Take Picasso's 'Faun in a Mauve Jumper,' which he painted in 1946. Raffaella, the Picasso please. Hardly likely that you would call it beautiful. Put it against a painting of the high Renaissance. Choose a painting, Raffaella. You will see that the aims, the purposes of a work of art have changed with the changing character of society. The definition of a work of art, then, must continuously be revised.

"I want for a moment to go back to the ancient Greeks, and talk about their sculpture. Slide please, Raffaella. Their gods and their heroes almost equally command our attention. Both behaved monstrously at times. Why were their gods like that? Against the sweet moderation of an Apollo, against their wise maxim 'Know thyself,' we have the frenzy of a Dionysus. Did Apollo represent the best side, Dionysus the underside, of a Mediterranean people subject to all the excitability and general drawbacks of a southern race? They began with this kind of statue. One or two slides of *kouroi,* please Raffaella. Note the Egyptian features, the frontal, dignified approach. Man as god. Dignity and remoteness are what the sculptor wants to emphasise. The Greek sculptor progressed, through the classical period, to this sort of purity. The Ludovisi throne, Raffaella."

Most of the ladies had seen this, and found it a welcome respite after the alien simperings of the Greek archaic statues.

"Now Raffaella, the fourth-century Praxiteles statue. How human is the emphasis by now—human, not divine . . ."

"The strength, the power . . ." muttered Juliette, in Doris's ear.

"Mmm. Pack a good punch, wouldn't he?" returned Doris Boot.

"Good heavens, it's nearly seven-thirty and I should have let you go ages ago!" Dr. Mowbray sounded surprised. "Before we break up, I'd like to recite Keats's famous 'Ode on a Grecian Urn.' I would like you to ponder a little, before we meet next week, on that line, so often discussed, 'Beauty is truth, truth beauty . . .' "

The lights were suddenly turned down still further, and the words of that exquisite poem, movingly articulated, floated with startling effect across the darkness to Mowbray's listeners.

"Thou still unravished bride of quietness,
    Thou foster-child of Silence and slow Time,
  Sylvan historian, who canst thus express
    A flowery tale more sweetly than our rhyme . . ."

Dr. Mowbray, having skilfully led his audience to a high pitch of emotion and left them with a lively wish, however short-lived, for knowledge and a determination for enquiry, abruptly stopped his lecture. He had played on their minds and emotions. Now they could go off and puzzle out what constituted a work of art. He wondered what nonsense they would come up with.

"Dear ladies, those of you who need not rush away, pray let Raffaella give you some refreshment. Glasses on the table over there."

"How excellent are your slides." Juliette, resolutely presenting her back to Raffaella, addressed Dr. Mowbray. "They speak, these statues, do you not agree?" She clutched Doris Boot's arm as she talked. "The artist speaks to us across the centuries, even if we do not always know his name."

Dr. Mowbray smiled warmly at her.

"He has a wealth of things to tell us, Madame." He threw a casual glance at those women standing near. "He speaks, but mutely, as you say. Without a name. The epistle is unsigned, the message—none the less telling for that—remains anonymous."

He took from his pocket suddenly an envelope and turned it over, frowning. He wondered once more about the nature of an anonymous letter-writer and his eyes played over the group. Probably a woman.

She would have a special sort of face, wouldn't she—warped, waspish, essentially ill-natured? One by one they passed under his inspection—that silent, wayward and secretive pair, Beverley Backhouse and Hedda Hardegen—Beverley with the face of a Leonardo angel, richly cream and gold in her black velvet jacket, Hedda pale and withdrawn as one of Botticelli's Graces, showing now a brooding intensity; Lady Loftus, whom no one had ever wanted to paint, the ingenuous round American face of wealthy Jo Ann Partridge . . . and his gaze came to rest on the small dark woman beside Juliette with the thin mouth and the sharp eyes. Mowbray knew her by now as Doris Boot. He would believe anything of *her.* He had even caught her nosing around in that sanctum sanctorum his study before the lecture. He'd forgotten to lock the door for once, and there she was, odious little busybody . . . actually kneeling on the floor to get a better look at that newly delivered painting of Branston's, which was propped up against the wall.

After the last of his group had departed that evening, Mowbray entered his study and stopped short. Raffaella was sitting in an armchair doing nothing.

"Good Lord, Masaccio's Madonna. That one . . . where is it? National Gallery in London, of course. You need only the Bambino to complete the pose."

As there was no response from her, he continued.

"I suppose we might eat. I don't know whether they were more mystified or impressed. How did it sound to you?"

She shrugged. "You were . . . performing brilliantly, as always."

"Thank you, m'dear. I thought it went off well myself. You disappear rather early, though. It would be so helpful if I didn't have to go on overtaxing my voice for another half-hour or so. Incidentally, we're nearly out of Scotch."

"Charles," she said suddenly. "There won't be any more duty-free Scotch. I have been *licenziata.*"

"What? Lost your job at the Consortium? Why?"

"I do not know."

"Incredible, after all the years you've been there. You'll find another job, of course, though I doubt you'll get anything as well paid. We'll feel the pinch, I suppose, until you get settled in something else. My new book will bring us some money, but the sale will be limited. This apartment is so expensive—"

She compressed her lips.

"I shan't be a burden on you . . ." she began, and fell silent as he said casually:

"I suppose the reason for your losing your job couldn't have anything to do with this, could it?"

He gave her an envelope, and watched while she extracted the single sheet of paper. Her hand flew to her mouth and she made a strangled sound.

"There, there, don't worry your pretty head. Perhaps you could both be a little more discreet in future, eh? Come, Raffaella, don't look as though the end of the world has come. We're both civilised people, I hope. I'm getting on, and I've decided to spare us the conventional frenzy of jealousy. No doubt your analyst recommended a little affair of the heart, am I right? What about something to eat, eh?"

"Charles, please, please listen one moment."

He sighed, and regarded her without expression.

"Charles, I wish . . . to leave you."

He became very still.

"You wish to what?"

Her lips tightened; she rose to her feet, with all the considerable dignity at her command, and walked to the window, where she paused, and then swung round, regarding him gravely.

"I wish to separate from you."

"Oh, not really, Raffaella! You mustn't take things so hard. Where would you go, and why on earth do you *want* to go?"

"I wish to go home to Mamma for a while first . . ."

"Go home to your mother? And what on earth would you do up in Modena? Mind you, the cathedral is one of the glories of Italy, certainly, but you can't spend all your time in the cathedral. Your mother is living in very reduced circumstances, too."

"Charles, do you not *realise* what I say?"

"Well, I'm not quite deaf yet, my dear. You say you want to leave me. Permanently?"

"Yes, Charles."

"For Backhouse?"

She was silent for a long time.

"And who else?"

"But in this case why leave *me?* I have just told you there is no need to feel badly about it. Very natural you should—er—want to kick over the traces a bit at your age. But what the devil happens if you go to him? He's a married man, with responsibilities."

"He wishes . . . he would marry me."

"What! You want to marry him?" Mowbray's voice rose on a note of sheer incredulousness. "You can't mean it. Backhouse! Good Lord, Raffaella, what do you see in the chap? Why, he doesn't know one painting from another. And then you talk of leaving *me* to marry *him!* No, you're not serious."

"You make a joke of everything," she said bitterly.

"Indeed I don't. It's no laughing matter. I suppose you haven't forgotten the fact that he's got a wife. What does she think of all this? We'll take it for granted she doesn't understand him, but will she divorce him?"

"This is no concern of yours, Charles."

"Oh come now, of course it is, you silly little girl. Now please be careful, Raffaella, you nearly knocked over the Apollo then."

Mowbray's voice expressed real concern for the first time as he hastened to pick up the little archaic statue with its proud gaze and geometric flat lines.

Raffaella uttered a cry and her voice trembled.

"You, your Apollo, your art, your paintings. You care for nothing, nothing else on earth. I once thought you capable of human relationships. But you are not human! You are cold, callous!"

She made to rush from the study, but Mowbray grasped her by the shoulders and forced her round to face him.

"Let's not do anything in a hurry," he said, his voice gentle now. "Backhouse is no longer a young man and you don't *know* his wife will divorce him. Raffaella, you can do this much for me. If, after another three months, you are still quite certain of your feelings for him and there are definite commitments from him, then I'll raise no objections. But meantime I want you to stop seeing him. Afterwards, if you both feel the same we'll face it calmly and see what can be done for the good of us all."

She was silent, breathing hard, and then said:

"Very well, Charles."

Without another look at him she left the room.

Alone, Mowbray stood quite still, looking at the closed door. Then suddenly he raised his arms as though in supplication. Then abruptly dropped them and flung round to his desk. Blindly he grasped the first object his hand touched and hurled it to the floor. It wasn't the Apollo, but it was a Nymphenburg porcelain which he valued nearly as much and it was reduced to atoms.

Behind the Scenes

IV

At a lazy and nostalgic hour of a February evening, Beverley, treading a reckless path, strolled with André Van Dam along the *passeggiata* at the top of the Spanish Steps, with many stops to look out over the roof-tops of Rome, now delicately illumined.

"Corot," said André.

"Almost. He did do one from here."

A group of Roman louts swaggering nearby leered at Beverley. André immediately placed himself between her and the Italians, throwing a protective arm round her shoulders. Something in his bearing made the men decide to move smartly off.

"I grew up here." Beverley's voice sang sadly. "It's so different now—political violence, Red Brigadists, kidnappings, a magistrate knocked off every second week, to say nothing of ordinary crime . . ."

"Got your gun tonight?"

"Don't laugh. It's no fun for a girl . . ."

"You didn't carry it last night."

"I had you instead."

Together, they had danced till three in the morning in a dive in Trastevere, locked together in the sweetness and violence of a three-man band. She glanced sideways at him now. His pursuit of her had been immediate and determined. Used as she was to such manoeuvres, she still felt a faint surprise.

Reading her thoughts in uncanny fashion, André ran a hand down her back and said:

"Does Hedda know you're out?"

Beverley stiffened. In her simple philosophy conscience never pricked unless with exposure; she was innocent until proved guilty. She suddenly rounded on Van Dam fiercely:

"Leave her out of it!"

André's grip tightened cruelly on her waist and a muscle twitched in his cheek.

"Behave yourself." His voice was harsh.

Beverley slumped.

After a while he asked: "At school together in England, were you?"

"All through. Our fathers were Rome-based diplomats," she answered absently.

"And you both got married straight out of school?"

"I told you before. Both of us," Beverley returned broodingly. "To men in the Consortium."

A wind rustled the ilexes overhead and Beverley shivered. She stopped and leaned on the balustrade. San Pietro gleamed like a star on the horizon, and the domes of some of Rome's six hundred churches floated lightly over the roof-tops.

"Are you going to take me to San Donato?" Van Dam leaned his hard bulky body beside her. Aggression seemed to flow from him. His hands, spread out now on the balustrade, were big and capable.

"If you want to. I'll ask Dr. Mowbray." Beverley's eyes were on the hands.

"I want to. Who's going?"

"Juliette Deneuve, for one."

"Oh Lord, is *she* going?"

"Yes. Are you buying much of her stuff?"

"Quite a few pictures. Am I coming home with you?"

"No. My husband is due in from Tripoli at eight o'clock."

"I'll put you in a cab now, then."

"Oh, it doesn't matter. He'll be met by . . . a Consortium car. I hardly see him nowadays," said Beverley, very brightly and carelessly.

"In that case, there's my suite at the Hassler. We might put in an hour."

"Oh? What for?" she asked stupidly, mesmerised still.

Brutally and explicitly, he told her what for.

John Backhouse, tall and arrogant, stood with his back to the window of the *pied-à-terre* which he had rented for some time in the Trastevere quarter of Rome. Raffaella sat on the bed.

"The devil of it is," said Backhouse, "there's no redress. I can't deny that from now on I need an Arabic-speaking assistant. We're shifting more and more business to the Arab world. It's where the richest investment projects are found now. Hardegen had a nerve to sack you in my absence, but you know the Consortium local staff has always been ruthlessly kept to a highly functional bare minimum."

Raffaella was silent, her head bowed.

"So your husband knows about me," Backhouse said suddenly.

She raised her eyes.

"Yes. I wish now I had told him long ago. I wish he had not learned first through an anonymous letter."

Backhouse started violently and barked so harshly that she jumped.

"What!"

"Someone wrote one about us."

Backhouse's face was very angry.

"*These* days! It's crazy. Crazy. Someone in the office, I'll be bound. Some resentful bastard who wants to get at me. Or one of the women who envy you."

Raffaella shivered.

"John, I feel frightened. Your . . . Beverley. She knows?"

"Eh?" Backhouse swung round and stared out of the window for a moment or two. "I haven't told her about you. In a strange sort of way, you see, you and she are quite separate."

"She agrees to a divorce?"

"Of course."

He turned and, bending over her, kissed her lips.

"Don't worry about all this. Oh, I almost forgot. *Un piccolo regalo per la più bella donna di Roma,"* he added ponderously, and did not notice she shuddered slightly at his pronunciation. He fumbled in his pocket and brought out a flat case.

"For me?" Raffaella faltered, as he opened it to reveal the

sparkling contents. "Oh John, how beautiful. A pendant and ear-rings to match. Oh John . . ."

"I can't give you a ring yet, my dear," he said simply.

He watched as she examined the stones one by one.

"John," she said presently. "I have told Charles, you know, that we . . . that we wish to marry."

Backhouse stiffened.

"Ah-ha. And?"

"He says to wait, for three or four months, to make sure that I will then think, then wish the same. . . ."

Backhouse's lips tightened.

"And . . . will you, I wonder? Feel the same?"

"Do you not . . . trust me, then?"

"Raffaella," he said thickly. "I trust you, by God I trust you." Putting his head down, he buried his face in her neck, while she stroked his hair, very gently, so as not to disturb the strands covering the balding patch.

"Oh Raffaella," he said. "You're the love of my life."

But only one week later, on another evening, stolen and secretive, Renato Barbicinti pulled up his Alfa in a secluded spot on the Janiculum Hill and looked at Raffaella, who sat beside him.

"Raffaella!" His voice was low and his eyes searched her face. "Raffaella! *Quanto tempo che non ti vedo più.* You do not begrudge me half an hour now and then, after so long?"

"It is—a long time," she admitted, her eyes dropping before him.

"It is precisely five years, eleven months and some days," he said crisply. "You were married on the tenth of May."

"Renato," her voice broke. "Don't, please don't."

"I will, then, speak of anything else in the world. The view, which we cannot see very well at the moment, or the paintings of Juliette Deneuve which you so roundly condemned in my gallery, or those three old men busy discussing the latest *crisi del governo*—so satisfactory a conversation is it that they all talk at once without pause—or that great sculptured cloud which has just sailed up over Trastevere . . . Which would you prefer?"

"The cloud, perhaps."

"It contains inside it Venus, that pink cloud, who watches over all beautiful women." His eyes laughed into hers.

Raffaella's defences were suddenly down.

"Oh Renato," she faltered. "You must go away. I can't bear it. I can't bear it!"

Beverley, like a slinky cat in her tight black pants, stretched luxuriously on a pile of cushions in her sitting room. The place shivered with fierce pounding rhythm. Hedda, restlessly prowling, uttered an exclamation and switched the record-player off. The silence was startling.

"What's wrong with you, Hed?"

"Every single time I've phoned you these last few days you've been out. That's what's wrong with me," burst out the other girl.

"You've been busy with Rudolf's aunt."

"She's gone now. I'm free for the afternoon. Now you tell me you're going out with that man you met in the Gianicolo. Van what's-his-name . . ."

"Van Dam."

"Have you been seeing him?"

"Of course not. He only rang up this morning and—"

"How did he know your number?"

"I suppose he looked it up in the phone book."

"I didn't like him."

"I could see that."

"You don't even know him!"

"He's a fellow Australian. I guess he's lonely." Beverley paused. "He said if I go to England he could probably find me a job. He knows loads of people there."

"You're not going to England!"

Beverley shrugged. "I think . . . John's plucking up courage to ditch me."

"What makes you think that?"

"Things he says . . ." said Beverley vaguely.

"You're imagining it."

Beverley said nothing. Hedda knelt down and took Beverley's face between her hands.

"Don't have anything to do with this Dutchman. Promise."

"Well, as a matter of fact," said Beverley, with hesitation, "you're going to give him a lift to San Donato along with me."

Hedda's hands dropped and she sprang up.

"Oh no!" She was horrified. She retreated several paces.

"I promised, Heddy. It's only a car ride." Beverley got up and sidled over.

"I'm not taking him. Anyway, he's not even in the class. You can't take him."

"I asked Professor Mowbray and he said it was all right."

Hedda looked stonily at her.

"Put him off. And tell him you're not going out this afternoon," she ordered.

"I can't *now.*" Beverley put her arms round Hedda and rubbed her face against hers. "There's absolutely no reason for jealousy," she murmured. "It's a passing thing."

Hedda uttered a cry and broke away. Beverley added hurriedly:

"Look, let's *all* go out this afternoon. We could all go out in the Lancia. Maybe go in the country and do some shooting practice."

"Oh yes! With that target of course."

Beverley smiled placatingly.

"Of course not. Not with André there."

"It's sick. D'you hear? It's off." Hedda's voice held suppressed violence.

"Calm down. We'll just all go out in the country then, Heddy."

"Oh yes." Hedda's voice broke. She was on the rack. "All of us. A happy trio. No thanks!"

For a second she gazed stormily at Beverley. Then she swung round and fled from the apartment, slamming the front door behind her with force enough to make the ornaments on the marble console rattle madly.

A few evenings later, Raffaella crept into the Palazzo Doria apartment and gained her own room without Mowbray hearing her. She sank into a chair and her head dropped forward into her hands.

A moment of truth came to her as it comes to all occasionally.

Unbidden and swift, a rush of dangerous thoughts were launching a deadly attack on that self-image which she was accustomed to consider her true one. Her motives and behaviour, polished up and ranged in strong ranks for self-inspection, had not stood fire, and were tottering, and all at the sight once more —two secret meetings, to be exact—of Renato Barbicinti. How would it have gone, marriage with him? He was penniless. But oh—Raffaella almost groaned aloud—how very attractive. Now more so than ever. How handsome, how amusing, how his voice caressed her, how immediate was the sympathy between them. And how comfortingly of an age with herself.

A brief affair? How dangerous and exciting. How well she remembered . . . Suddenly the onslaught was complete and Raffaella's lips twisted, trembled in a wide reminiscent smile, and her eyes shone. For a long time she sat there, recklessly surrendering herself to remembered, forbidden joy. Then she uttered a cry and, springing up, paced the floor. God, what was she thinking of? These romantic dreams. What did she want with them, when John showered her with attention? Dear John. There was nothing he would not do for her. With one hand she fingered, beneath her blouse, the handsome pendant he had brought back. Heaven knew how much he had paid for it. Far too much, no doubt, as he was always taken in by vendors in such matters. It would have cost five million lire in Rome. She knew, because already she had had it valued.

Stage Set

V

Three weeks later, some hundred and fifty kilometres east of
Rome, Charles Mowbray and Renato Barbicinti stood outlined
against the sky, on the edge of a wall of rock. In front of them
the Monti Simbruini, grim and magnificent, glowed purple in
the late afternoon light. A panorama of mile upon mile
stretched before them of sky and mountain and ravine, wooded
yet desolate. Behind them was San Donato, the remains of an
ancient Benedictine monastery high above, and some thirteen
kilometres removed from the parent monastery of San Benedetto.

"Unpaintable. A Turner or a Corot might get a suggestion of
the light, but how deal with the grandeur?"

Mowbray's voice was excited, and the Italian was quick to
respond.

"There are no limitations to them. They are . . ." He flung
back his rich curls. ". . . beyond description." He laughed.
"What a setting for lectures."

Mowbray nodded.

"Can I live up to them, I wonder?"

It was not to be one lecture, but a series of lectures—extraordinary.

"Saint Benedict founded twelve monasteries in the area,"
Mowbray had told his class. "Like San Benedetto itself, San
Donato is cut out of the rock, but has been buried for several
centuries owing to a landslide and was virtually forgotten about.
When the stuff was cleared away recently, little of the monastery remained. But they discovered extensive fresco painting in
what had been the lower church—very probably the work of

two very famous painters. The local authorities have done the place up and will admit the public during the coming summer. It is still officially closed, but I might be able to make arrangements to take a group up there. You will have a preview."

The two men gazed for a moment in silence before Barbicinti looked down the hill and said:

"Here comes Mr. Tsuda."

"Ah, the gentleman of the Mercedes parked down below?"

"Yes."

They turned to watch a Japanese gentleman walking towards them.

"One solitary Jap looks out of place," commented Mowbray. "You feel he has escaped from his tourist bus."

"Raffaella said the Belle Arti people asked if he could join us."

"That's so," agreed Mowbray. "I wasn't there when they telephoned. Now what will *he* make of the frescoes?"

"Two painters little known outside Italy . . ."

"Mr. Tsuda?" Mowbray swung round. "Ah, delighted to welcome you, sir."

Mr. Tsuda bowed. He was fairly short, pencil slim and exquisitely tailored in dark wool. His skin was lighter in colour than that of most Japanese and his spectacles glinted red in the sunlight. Behind them his eyes were dark and impassive.

"Tell me," pursued Mowbray, "how did you know about San Donato?"

"My ambassador in Rome is a personal friend. He hears of such things. And Lorenzo Monaco is a painter I find wholly fascinating." Mr. Tsuda smiled. He had a ready smile, confined to his mouth. "These swaying figures of Lorenzo's—what grace they have, what sinuous rhythm, how seductive these Gothic lines. I have been to the Santa Trinità in Firenze and seen Lorenzo's Story of the Virgin frescoes and the Annunciation altar-piece. Tell me, why did *he* do them, and not Masaccio—so new and so startling?" He smiled again, insinuatingly.

"The Bankers' Guild chose him." Mowbray stared at Tsuda. "Upper-class people. They didn't want Masaccio. He was too radical, too progressive."

"Here comes your ladies." Barbicinti laid a hand on Mowbray's arm.

"What? Oh . . . Ah . . ." Mowbray allowed himself to be drawn away. "We'll continue this discussion later," he said regretfully.

"I shall be honoured," Tsuda bowed again. "I have not, by the way, been able to find the curator."

"He's not here," Mowbray called over his shoulder. "The Belle Arti people in Rome gave him permission to entrust me with the keys to the lower level. Quite unofficially, of course." As they hurried up the steps he muttered to Barbicinti: "That chap knows painting—more than any of this lot!"

They had all arrived now: Lady Loftus, with her faithful shadow Marjorie Bennett; Juliette Deneuve, who had, simply because they had chanced to sit beside one another in the Rome lectures, given a lift to the little Yorkshirewoman Doris Boot; the Americans Jo Ann Partridge and Louise Parsons; and Beverley Backhouse and Hedda Hardegen, who had brought the Dutchman Van Dam.

Mowbray looked at Juliette with love. Of all the class she had always been the most truly receptive, but he thought a hundred times more of her since Vicovaro, where they had stopped on the way up. There he had seen her put the finishing touches to a painting of the shimmering green valley of the River Aniene with its olives and vines, and the Monti Prenestini gleaming in the west. Her handling of all the lovely flickering light up the valley, the depth she had got, had impressed him. And he had told her so . . .

Thank God for Juliette. To her he directed his lectures now, to her alone. Those accursed women, accursed unattractive rich women—always excepting that decorative pair Hedda and her friend Beverley; though you would never know what they were thinking. Beverley—Backhouse's wife! Who, by Jove, carried a gun in her handbag!

Up on the outside terrace he addressed his group, drawing forward a swarthy Italian couple. "Here are Augusto and Lucia. They will look after us for our stay here. Even if Augusto is a silent fellow, Lucia makes up for him. Her family have been in these parts for generations and she is full of tale and superstition. They are the only people on hand here for the week-end. The official curator-designate has not yet taken up his duties."

Augusto was a spare, dark man who looked like Julius Caesar, his wife a tough little brown-faced peasant, voluble and loud-voiced, who picked up Juliette's heavy wooden painting equipment as though it were made of straw and looked around for more to carry.

"You'll have noticed the renovations," continued Mowbray. "The whole of the entrance passage here had crumbled away over time. Yes, Lady Loftus, it was over there that the landslide occurred. San Donato was once a monastery of a fair size. Only a part of it remains. But a part with very considerable attractions, as you will see."

Mowbray had pushed open an incongruously modern door and ushered his flock into the interior. Eagerly, they filed in, stumbling through a rude vestibule and down rough, steep steps into what seemed near darkness.

"Well, I thought we'd come to enjoy the light effects," muttered Jo Ann Partridge to her next-door neighbour, whom she could not see.

"You are standing," Mowbray's voice, thin and remote now, sounded in their ears, "in the upper church of the former abbey of San Donato, constructed we don't know exactly when, though probably about 1350. The landslide carried off the outer entrance and nearly all the residential quarters, but left intact this series of chapels. I'll open the doors again now."

Their eyes were now accustomed to the interior light. A glow all about them took on shape and form. They were in a lofty cavern, gleaming with colour, alive with shimmering figures. On one side, panels told the story of the Nativity and Marriage of the Virgin, on the other the life of Christ.

"You see in front of you one of the loveliest works of the early Quattrocento."

They looked in silence on the glowing colours, on the delicate, mobile faces of fifteenth-century Florentines masquerading as the Holy Family, at the gracious fall of rich robes, at the tracery of distant foliage and slender pillars backed by the hills and vines and olives of Tuscany, the whole set against a sky of gentlest blue.

"They are—I am certain—the work of Lorenzo Monaco." Mowbray's voice was eager. "He was not known to have worked up here. But I would say that the Story of the Virgin belongs almost certainly to his last years. Tomorrow you can look at these frescoes at your leisure, but this evening you have seen them at their best. Delightful, aren't they? Really delightful."

His class, swayed by the enthusiasm which throbbed in Mowbray's voice, all superciliousness gone, and by the extreme pull of the paintings, whose gilded colours danced now in the rays of the setting sun, smiled on him and on those enchanting figures, who reached out to these fresh visitors of a new age with the same insistent charm as when first created five centuries before.

The group was led up and down stairs, through a maze of small chapels and shrines. Often the rock lay bare. Candles, lit specially for them, revealed the lives of those holy men: Benedict himself, now crudely drawn, now severe and stylised after the early Byzantine period. On all sides the saints of the order looked down: Benedict, Gregory the Great, the Archdeacon Peter, Romanus, Maurus, Placidus, Honoratus, Scholastica and Anatolia.

Finally, to what had been the sacristy, where sixteen frescoes of the legend of Saint Benedict lined the walls.

"Spinello Aretino," explained Mowbray excitedly, "without a doubt. You may remember he once decorated the sacristy of San Miniato in Florence with just such an array of frescoes. He did those about 1387 or so. The Benedictines commissioned a great many works of art. Now here Spinello's style is still a very peculiar mixture of the old and the new. Let me explain . . ."

Back in Rome, John Backhouse descended from the Consortium limousine in front of his apartment block in Via Guerrieri. Then, picking up a suitcase, attaché case and raincoat, he made his way inside. In the marble entrance hall he was caught by the *portiera*.

"*Buongiorno, Signor Backhouse, ben tornato!*"

He mumbled a greeting, hoping the woman would not begin her usual stream of inanities. She was saying something now about the *"signora"* and *"ieri mattina."* It seemed that Beverley was away for the weekend. Backhouse stared at the woman. She was still mouthing away? What now? The robbery, the rape— the porter indicated a morning paper. Backhouse had glanced over the same edition on his way in from Fiumicino. It had been just up Via Guerrieri—the sort of street to attract trouble, lined with luxurious apartment blocks and one or two big villas. He wondered if Beverley ever carried her gun these days and thought how the porter's eyes would pop if he mentioned it.

Thankfully, he pressed the lift button, shooting up to the first floor. He had never got the hang of the Italian language. They all spoke too fast; and the faster they talked, the more they yelled. Awful. But he was beginning to make progress with his lessons in Arabic.

In the entrance hall he saw an envelope in Beverley's writing on the console. It was addressed to him. Instead of opening it, he took his stuff through to his bedroom, threw off his jacket and, picking up his mail, went into the lounge and poured himself a drink.

He had settled down with his letters when he remembered Beverley's note. Oh hell, he'd look at it presently. He was not thinking of her. Did not want to think of her. He had been thinking of Raffaella nearly all the way back from Africa. How she dominated his leisure hours now. Madness? Oh God—John Backhouse groaned to himself—did he make himself ridiculous? He would ring Raffaella now. The meeting in Morocco had been hectic, though the results were satisfactory. No time to think about personal problems . . .

What would Raffaella be doing now, the darling? Lighting a cigarette, he settled down at the telephone and dialled her number. No reply. Where on earth was she? Curse it, if she were out for the day, he might not see her till heaven knew when. Moodily, all his eager anticipation dampened, he went out to the balcony. Damn it all, and with Beverley away . . .

What did Beverley think of it all? When he had talked to her of divorce, she had agreed almost light-heartedly. He had been almost affronted. As though she didn't care a damn. But he thought she cared very much. She had been so full of gaiety lately, but in a strange, feverish way. Now that he was no longer in her power, he felt sorry for her, beautiful as she was, caught in the toils of her own unbridled sexuality. He also knew she loved him, in her own way.

A picture of Beverley came, all spontaneously, before him—

that face and form which had once held such enchantment, nine years ago. He had been thirty-seven, seventeen years older. . . . Then Hedda Hardegen, married too, within the year. It had been so providential, the two girls kept saying, happening to marry men in the same city, in the same office. Providential for them. Sometimes Backhouse looked at Hardegen and wondered what *he* thought and felt.

The letter. He got it and tore it open. Subiaco. She had gone to Subiaco, with the others attending that art course. "If I'm not back Tuesday morning," she had written, "I will probably have gone further afield with Hedda. This time the Mowbrays are taking the class to a deserted monastery, the old San Donato, to look at the frescoes. San Donato is just beyond Subiaco."

"The Mowbrays." Both of them, then. Of course Raffaella would have had to go. Old Mowbray always had her around when the lectures were on. Despite himself, John Backhouse's heart sank. To have hurried back like this a day early all for nothing. He wondered moodily what he would do with himself for the rest of the day. He needed a break after ten days' frantic pressure. He might try that golf course up at Punt'Ala he had been told about.

He shaved, showered, inspected his profile in the mirror. What a gut he was getting with all this travelling, all these business dinners and rich food. On an impulse he went into the kitchen and made himself a sandwich. Today he would miss out on lunch. He put out his clubs. Yes, Punt'Ala. A nice drive on a fine day. He'd get in an afternoon's golf and sleep up there overnight. He might take the Via Aurelia. Not been on it for years. He looked out a road map, and picked up a copy of *The Economist* and *The Daily American* he had bought that morning.

Suddenly he thought of the robbery further up Via Guerrieri, and it occurred to him to check on Beverley's gun. He opened the door of her bedroom. A strange sensation it was. It seemed like intruding, after all this time. He went over to the bedside table where Beverley kept the little automatic at night and, throwing the papers on the bed, opened a drawer. The gun was gone. But there was something else there which sent his heart cold. The cardboard rectangle had once been a photograph of

Raffaella. But that was before it had been used as a target. Now it was peppered with bullet holes.

Frozen, he stood there a long time. Beverley was crazy. Crazy, and he thought she had been drinking lately too.

"Oh, good Christ," he groaned.

Ten minutes later, he was at the wheel of his BMW, threading his way impatiently through the jumble of traffic on the Via Cristoforo Colombo, which would lead him to the Raccordo Anulare and the shortest possible way east towards Subiaco.

"It would be impossible," said Dr. Mowbray, who had led his group up to the big hall when the sun went down, "to overestimate the importance which religion played in the life of medieval man. The age of faith is hardly comprehensible to us sceptics. It was belief in the power of God and the necessity of prayer that sent Saint Benedict here and caused him to found the first Benedictine communities. You have had a little trouble getting here, a little inconvenience . . ." Mowbray's voice was light and a protesting murmur rose from his audience. ". . . but you cannot, any of you, have failed to be impressed by the lofty splendour of your surroundings."

Another murmur rose from the ladies, which Mowbray skilfully ignored.

"What a place," his voice rang out. "What a place for the anchorites of old to have chosen." Here Mowbray's eyes moved to the tall arched window of the hall, which gave a last prospect of the mountains, darkening before the oncoming storm. "A place where all the limitations and inconsequences of everyday, chattering life fall away from us.

"And just because we are here, first-comers for a very long time, in a place so redolent of faith, I wonder if you fully comprehend the role, in such an age, of a body of men utterly convinced of the power, of the efficacy, of prayer. They took the vows of obedience, of chastity, of poverty—and thus sought to fling off the bonds of earthly existence. Their worship was continuous—worship and prayer, for the benefit of us all. Their lives were devoted to the worship of God, the salvation of their souls and the souls of their fellows. We can imagine how other men of their day felt towards the monks of the Middle Ages, the value placed by the rest of the community on them, whose lives were spent seeking these priceless benefits from God, on behalf of their fellows."

The gathering darkness, only faintly pierced by candles, was suddenly torn by a brilliant flash of lightning from the tall arched windows, followed almost immediately by a tremendous crash of thunder.

"It is six o'clock," pointed out Mowbray. "The hour of Compline, the office that finished the monastic day. You might expect to see the shades in this hall, mightn't you, of the monks of old, in their white cowls . . ."

A wind suddenly whistled through the hall, extinguishing the candles. One of the ladies whimpered. It was seen, then, that one lamp remained burning.

Mowbray's voice rang out.

"Compline was normally conducted in darkness, in fact with just one lamp to light the monk who read aloud from Benedict's rule.

"Fratres," he intoned, *"sobrii istote et vigilate, quia adversarius vester diabolus tanquam lea rugiens circuit quaerens quem devoret, cui resistite fortes in fide!**

"The terrors of the night were strong and real." Mowbray's voice was vibrant and powerful. "The final office sought to expel the evil spirits—"

Again came a blinding flash of lightning, and a woman screamed. Simultaneously, as Mowbray's voice died away and mingled with the subsequent sound of thunder, there arose from the shadows around them the powerful Gregorian chant, soaring upwards, rolling round and engulfing the little group, who huddled closer on their rude wooden chairs, while above them the heavens opened and the Devil aimed his thunder bolts.

"Well, I sure do think we deserve a little drop of something after all that." Mrs. Partridge's voice was more than ordinarily expressive as she sank down on her narrow bed in the cell assigned

* The source for the above paragraphs on the Benedictines is a delightful book by Patrick Leigh Fermor, *A Time to Keep Silence,* John Murray Publishers Ltd., 1957.

to her. The candle-light flickered fitfully in the draught from
the tall, narrow, pointed window and played strangely on the
rounded features of the American woman. "All that lecturing
straight on top of the drive up, without even time to wash our
hands . . ."

"It was a case of catching the light, of course," replied Louise
Parsons.

"It was terrifically dramatic. I for one was mighty impressed
with the build-up—phew, all the singing coming in suddenly. I
confess I thought it was real. I never knew he was bringing
taped music with him. All the same I think he might'uv checked
that the heating and facilities were a bit more adequate." Jo
Ann rummaged round in a carry-all as she spoke, producing
bottles and glasses.

"What about ice?"

"I reckon I've enough in the ice-box. Can't thaw in this temperature too quickly. You go get the other girls . . ."

"You better check. Can't make a Martini without ice, Jo Ann."

Jo Ann gave a loud, comforting hoot of laughter. "Sure can't."

"Waal, I'm glad we're *doing* something at last," said Louise. "I
just love all the culture in this country, as much as any of the
Englishwomen, but to listen to that old Kipling relic of the
colonial age (and you know who I mean), you'd think she and
her friends had an option on it all."

Hedda, sitting on Beverley's narrow bed in the semi-darkness,
looked at the narrow, whitewashed cell, with its plain stone
floor, its Gothic window. Only the thin mattress, the rough
sheets and blankets, a wooden stool and table, and a couple of
hooks set into the wall made any concession to a guest's wants.

The party had been conducted from the big hall where Mowbray had lectured, along a stone corridor and through a huge
iron door which cut the monks' cells off from the rest of the
monastery. On one side of a passageway lay a row of identical
cells, at the end the simplest of washrooms, and that was all.
What were the Americans saying to the lack of a shower, of
proper heating?

Hedda, rising to her feet, leaned on the window-shelf formed
by the setting in of the window to a foot-thick stone wall. Out-

side was blackness and the wildness of the storm and often there would come a flash of lightning. Turning, her eyes roamed over Beverley's open overnight bag, its contents carelessly scattered around, handbag and jacket flung down beside them.

Ten minutes later Beverley threw open the door and started back as thunder rumbled ominously about the old building. As lightning threw its white brilliance on her slender form, she pretended to shiver in terror, then struck an attitude, her back to the wall, her hands outspread. Then she relaxed and began to execute a series of dance steps.

"Jo Ann's making Martinis. Want to join her?" asked Hedda.

Still dancing, Beverley executed a last pirouette and collapsed on the bed.

"Martinis," she gurgled. "How deliciously . . . inappropriate."

Hedda was silent. Beverley saw the alarm in her eyes and subsided, hanging her head. "I was only exorcising the bad spirits, Heddy." She rummaged in her handbag for a cigarette.

"Any drink is better than nothing on a night like this . . ." Hedda's voice died away as she saw the other girl's sudden immobility. Beverley raised her eyes slowly to Hedda.

"My gun's gone."

Hedda said nothing.

"My gun's gone, Heddy, gone out of my purse. What've you done with it?"

"Why do you think I took it?"

"Hedda! Why have you taken my gun?"

"Beverley! Stop this. Stop it! . . . I didn't, I didn't, do you hear?"

In the big hall, Mowbray crouched over the slide projector, giving directions now imperious, now testy, to Raffaella, who moved back and forth fetching screwdrivers, extra flex, or lamps. There was electric current, generator provided, only in the big hall and kitchen region, and sadly inadequate for their purpose.

Renato stood observing the pair, his eyes fixed on Raffaella. A sinuous but strong grace animated those splendid limbs. What a pleasure to watch her as she moved about, clad now in a long flaring skirt, her blonde hair drawn up in a simple knot on her neck. How pleasant to see her out of those eternal pants all the women wore nowadays. Mowbray never would stop fussing. *Maledizione!* How dare he order her around like that! Raffaella —there was magic in that body, which he had heard someone once describe as heavy. Heavy! She had the body a woman should have, all grace and strength. Not another woman here tonight to touch her, with perhaps the exception of the Deneuve. She, he must admit, had something of the same attraction, though more blatant and less appealing, with her dyed hair and her trinkets.

"I think this will work all right now." Mowbray, his head in the projector, did not see the mute appeal of Renato, the insistent gaze he directed at Raffaella, her sudden colouring.

Mowbray raised a heated face from his operations.

"Well, I'd best be off to change and brush up. Lucia will have dinner ready at seven; that's right, isn't it, Raffaella? You might tell her and Augusto to move the screen and all this stuff into the corner."

"Together, we will dispose of it. The servants are busy in the kitchen." Renato, with a light laugh, began to collect the various appurtenances of Mowbray's art.

"And I had better make myself presentable." Mowbray stretched his tall body and ran a hand through his white locks. He glanced at his watch and with muttered thanks to Renato made his way towards the door.

For a few moments the other two went silently through the work of clearing up, and then Renato laid a compelling hand on Raffaella's shoulder, forcing her gaze to meet his. With a slight motion of his head, he indicated the outside door. Still in silence and moved by a compulsion that was scarcely her own, she followed him outside.

VI

Beverley, entering the big hall before dinner, was joined by Van Dam and Doris Boot. Doris, clad tonight in black with a crimson scarf at her neck, was in high spirits.

"Jo Ann mixes a stiff drink. You missed a lively party."

If Van Dam left an unspoken question in the air, Doris was not slow to insinuate it.

"I suppose," she gave an alcoholic snigger, "our two *inseparables* enjoyed themselves in their own way."

Beverley gave her a horrified look. Doris continued, a shade defiantly:

"André and I had a most interesting discussion about Venetian painting. I've been filling him in on our lectures."

Beverley smiled dangerously and said distinctly:

"How simply marvellous for André."

Doris stared hard at her.

"Some of us haven't lived in this country all our lives like you have," she snapped. "It'd be a bit queer if you didn't know more about Italian painting than I do, wouldn't it?"

She turned abruptly and stalked off to the other side of the hall, where Raffaella was giving directions to Lucia.

Van Dam laughed, dismissing Doris with a slight shrug.

"You would have enjoyed Jo Ann's drinking session. None of the other men turned up. There I was, like . . . like—"

"Like a turkey cock among the sparrows?"

"All the less attractive sparrows too," he grinned.

"You wanted to come," returned Beverley indifferently.

"Oh, I did. You're an angel to have brought me," he assured her.

"There's your favourite sparrow over there now," she remarked coolly, indicating Raffaella.

With one hand Van Dam forced her round to face him.

"Oh, come off it." He was so close the cruel sensuous face was a pale blur.

Beverley kicked him on the ankle and wrenched herself neatly from his grasp.

"You've got what you wanted out of me," she said pleasantly. "So sod off."

She turned on her heel and walked indolently away.

"Life's overstepping the mark."

To John Backhouse, steering his BMW up the mountain, the words—whatever they might mean—kept recurring, an instinctive protest at a situation which by now had a nightmarish quality. He was on his way up the side of a mountain to stop his wife using a gun on—on Raffaella. Oh Lord, what a crazy, impossible idea. It *wasn't* possible, was it? She would not really use that little Walther, that pretty, lethal toy? Then why in the name of heaven had she taken it with her?

He had bought it for her himself, after their apartment had been twice broken into. He had always travelled continuously and she would be left alone on average six months of the year.

He was now back in the past, plucking one familiar picture after another from the album, reliving his crazy adulation of the first years, his own utter self-abasement to this girl—no, this child, rather, with yet such sophisticated sensuality—reliving his misery at the increasing frequency of her infidelities, and his final realisation of her passion for Hedda. What a fool he had been and how he had been duped. All the same, hadn't he become a sort of mainstay for her? A mainspring rather, helping to pull her together. An anchor. To say nothing of money and position. What would she do now, without him, this beautiful *amorale?* Intelligent of course, clever. Her mind played about in places where he could not always follow, practical type that he was. His face darkened as he thought how she had so often not listened to him while he talked. He had caught her out countless times.

Raffaella, now, was an excellent listener, intelligent and receptive. Raffaella, who was never moody, always sweet and pliant, with that golden skin of hers, that rich body that always reminded him of sculptured marble with the sun on it, who moreover adored him, on whom he could so utterly depend.

Gripping the wheel, John Backhouse urged the BMW on as fast as he dared, the wheels crunching now on the stony, crumbly surface. The sky was black, the storm near to breaking. Pencils of lightning flickered against the sombre backdrop, a vast blanket of humidity filled the world—evil, hostile, ominous. It was already six-thirty, and darkness was closing in. The headlamps played on overhanging masses of dark rock rejecting and threatening the rough road which wound now in a series of hairpins towards San Donato—at last visible as a tracery of shallow arches, a squat tower, a row of faintly gleaming windows, set into the mountain itself.

And if all was normal? How to explain his presence? John Backhouse's lips tightened grimly. Why worry about that? Prevention was all that mattered.

The wheels of the BMW crunched to a stop beside the other vehicles parked on the lower level of the old ruined complex, and Backhouse sat for a few moments collecting himself. His heart was beating painfully. Slowly, he climbed from his car and in the gathering darkness made his way up the steps leading to the upper level.

Thunder was rumbling all around and the first heavy drops of rain were falling. His rubber soles made no noise as he gained the last flight of steps, obviously newly cut, to the long, covered porch. All was in darkness, only a faint glow from the rose window overhead filtering out a little light from inside. Slowly, reluctantly now, he walked along the corridor. And then stopped dead.

A long, low, gurgling laugh came to his ears. A woman's laugh, gentle and deep-throated. Silence, and then a man's voice speaking Italian, though he could catch only a word or two here and there, and then the woman's, her words drawn from her in a long moan, "No, no, no", and then only indistinguishable sounds broke the silence until the woman spoke again, so low he could not hear, except for the two words which came vibrant and unmistakable, *"Ti amo."*

John Backhouse took two more steps forward. At first he made out nothing at all in the gloom, and then lightning briefly illumined the couple who clasped each other with frantic, passionate abandon. The man was young and slim and unknown to Backhouse. The blonde hair of the woman, her bubbling laughter, he would have known anywhere. It was Raffaella.

John Backhouse, having lived, it seemed to him, through aeons of time, turned abruptly and stumbled back along the corridor, down the steps in the direction of the lower courtyard and his car. His cheeks were wet with tears, though whether of rage or grief he could not tell.

All On Stage

VII

"I sure have a queer sensation this evening," said Jo Ann reflectively as she watched Lucia ladle pasta from an immense steaming bowl. "I have this feeling I'm living in a kind of a dream and none of this is real, perched up here on the side of the mountain, with only a tiny part of this old monastery left. I feel we might all be swept away too in the storm and not a sign of us left behind."

She started, as from far off came the swelling notes, the complex chanting of an unseen choir in the severe and august Gregorian, weaving its pattern now faintly, now insistently about the group of diners at the long refectory table. The table was lit by three groups of iron candelabra, and the outer reaches of the hall were engulfed in darkness. The storm still raged, the shriek of wind now added to the thunder of the rain.

"It's the feeling you get," continued Jo Ann, "when you poke your head out of that old archway over there, and you feel it should lead somewhere, for heaven's sake, but there's only a bit of rubble and the night, and, and . . . nothingness. Ugh."

"You've had a cocktail too many, Jo Ann," Louise Parsons said bluntly. "That's all that's wrong with you."

But she shivered, as there came from outside a thunderous crash, and lightning illumined the gathering eerily.

"Ah, the music." Juliette's soft brown eyes shone with excitement. "Our lecturer has the sure, dramatic touch, Signor Barbicinti. What an atmosphere! A never-to-be-forgotten sight, the frescoes of today, and what a setting for the lectures. Do you not agree?"

"Most certainly!" Renato's face reflected Juliette's enthusiasm. "A toast to Professor Mowbray!" He raised his voice and sprang to his feet, glass in hand. The chattering died away. "A toast to you, for your excellent idea in bringing us here, for your elegant addresses, for your unceasing efforts to entertain us." He laughed, the sound issuing softly from his throat. His eyes, roaming the table, avoided Raffaella.

"Very fine figure of a young man, isn't he?" murmured Lady Loftus appreciatively to Hedda, who sat beside her. "A little bit more than the normal *joie de vivre* tonight. That face. You'd never know what was really going on in that head of his, would you?"

"He is not so good looking as Dr. Mowbray must have been at that age," commented Jo Ann, regarding Mowbray, who was holding a conversation of elegant erudition with Mr. Tsuda. "He looks so well in that dark jacket and black tie. Dark hair goes white so beautifully of course, especially with black eyebrows and flashing eyes."

"Lovely teeth," added Doris. "His own too. Makes a big difference."

Lady Loftus shuddered and turned her back to Doris, who spoke to Jo Ann again.

"He's still a smasher, Mowbray. Wonder how long they've been married, those two."

"Five years or so, I believe."

"Fancy her marrying a man so much older."

"Waal, we noticed when we visited here some years ago that plenty of young girls were married to old men. Times were hard and it was a case of economic necessity. The young ones didn't have the money."

"How old would his wife be?"

"Early thirties, I guess," said Jo Ann. "Old-fashioned look to her somehow. She should lose some weight."

"Big in the beam."

Raffaella sat brooding in her seat. She had drunk more wine than usual but it hadn't banished fear or the memory of the previous afternoon. While her eyes passed from face to face round the table, she was back on the Jenne road, which they had all travelled the previous afternoon, that road that clung so precariously to the side of the mountain, snaking away here and there into a tunnel hewn through the rock. Above, the cliff-side threatened. *"Caduta massi"* warned the road signs. Falling boulders were a menace on that road . . .

And then once more she was standing on that giddy look-out point, long after the others had begun the winding descent. Half a kilometre below they had disappeared from view and the noise of their engines died. Charles had wanted her to precede him on the way down to Subiaco, but she had sent him off. Then for a long time she stared out over the gorge, glad to be entirely alone. Under way again, had she driven more carelessly than usual? Perhaps, so immersed had she been in her thoughts—feeling, besides, the confidence of a resolution taken, a resolution which allowed no further *arrière-pensée*. Yes, she'd felt confident—just before, with a screech of tyres, she had rounded a sharp curve. Approaching the next corner a little fast, her foot had gone down sharply on the brake pedal. Simultaneously the Simca had lurched and slid to the edge of the road. Panic-stricken, she had twisted the steering wheel, but the Simca had continued to pull violently towards the bank . . . Sweat suddenly broke out all over Raffaella's body, and her eyes pursued their feverish search of the faces about her . . . falling now on Beverley, so indolently beautiful—and hostile and, surely, frightened now, behind her hostility; now on Hedda, of the reckless eyes, who sat without a word; on Juliette, whose restless dark gaze so often turned on Raffaella when she thought Raffaella did not see. How she hated Raffaella for her remarks on her paintings: the one thing Juliette could never forgive. Now Raffaella surprised Charles looking at her. Charles had been full of concern for her since the accident to the Simca, but tonight—was he not too exquisitely polite to her tonight, to that degree which, she knew of old, spelt trouble?

But now Mowbray was talking, looking round the table for attention.

"I must explain," he raised his voice, "that after dinner we want you to leave this hall while we get it ready for the slides. It means retiring to your rooms for half an hour or so. Then we have a little surprise for you, thanks to Augusto. He tells me the monks of old were called to their Matins by an echo. One monk rang a bell out near the kitchen and it sounded through the rock quite clearly to the cells. Some acoustical quirk—perhaps a pattern of small natural fissures. We'll try it out for the nine-thirty lecture tonight. I would ask you all to be prompt. Mr. Tsuda, for one, will be leaving very early tomorrow morning. About five, I think you said, sir?"

"Another toast—to Lucia and Augusto!" Juliette also rose. There was a loud and hearty chorus in her support, while the Italian couple stood smiling and nodding.

"Lucky to find people to work so hard these days." Van Dam surveyed the laden table. "I'm surprised they can open up these frescoes at all, with the staff shortage and the strikes."

"The state of the frescoes here is quite reasonable, after the time they have been closed up," remarked Renato.

"At least they can't be stolen," put in Jo Ann. "You can damage a fresco but you can't roll it up and take it away. I suppose you all saw yesterday's *Messaggero?*"

"The theft at Urbino?"

"Two Piero della Francesca gone and also "La Muta" of Raffaella."

"The theft of 'La Muta' is a cruel blow indeed," said Mowbray. "The only Raffaello remaining in his native Urbino. Imagine her, 'La Muta,' ending up in a fat German's boudoir or some obscure gallery of the American Far West or—" automatically he fitted his words to his audience, as a lecturer will, "forlorn and alone in the Sydney Art Gallery, among the gum-trees and Ned Kellys." Mowbray laughed freely. "Or even in the concrete wilds of modern Tokyo." He swallowed some wine and beamed round the table, so completely unaware of having said anything that could possibly offend anyone that Jo Ann's tart words took him by surprise.

"I guess your Lord Elgin and all the young dandies of the Grand Tour days didn't share your sentiments."

Mowbray eyed her benevolently.

"They certainly had no more scruples than the curators of your immensely well stocked Metropolitan Museum, Mrs. Partridge. But 'La Muta' was so much part of Urbino that her loss is shocking. To snatch such a painting from its own setting is infamous."

"You surprise me." It was Raffaella, her voice trembling as she regarded Mowbray. "I thought you had other views."

"You're mistaken, then, my dear." Mowbray laughed. "I abhor the removal of a painting from its native soil. Perhaps you are thinking of what I was saying recently about the carelessness of the Italians with their works of art. But it is one of Italy's charms, of course, that they are so casual with them. They have such profusion they are unaccustomed to regard them with anything like the respect—the awe even—of less gifted nations like the Germans or Swiss or English. Though nowadays one wonders what the end will be, given the tremendous volume of tourists—bus load after bus load everywhere, the beautiful old marble and parquet floors groaning under their weight, their vulgar gaping cloying the very air. I would swear Botticelli's Venus looked tired the last time I saw her, soiled from the contact of unsympathetic eyes."

"The concrete wastes of Tokyo contain some oases, however, Professor." Mr. Tsuda giggled, quite unabashed. He was enjoying himself, beaming at Mowbray behind his spectacles. "I venture to say, more oases than Sydney can boast. We have a long culture, an unbroken art history going back for centuries past. I like to think, in our vulgarian world, that the private collector may be the sort of repository and guardian of art that the Benedictines were, as you said, for learning . . ."

Mr. Tsuda pursued this theme for some time, his words issuing forth in a silken stream. The threads were eventually severed by Jo Ann.

"I guess," her words dropped factually on all this romancing, "that private collectors will have to do just that if the Italians don't take more care of their stuff than they do at Urbino. Two guards at night for forty roomfuls of treasures."

"They even rob churches—" began Lady Loftus.

But Doris suddenly took command of the conversation, loudly and tipsily.

"Thirty thousand churches there are in this country," she stated solemnly. "It'd take a while to do that lot over."

She reached out for a decanter. Renato intercepted her, his face all spurious solicitude as he filled her glass for her.

"Ah," Juliette tittered nervously, "only two years ago, the

'Nativity' of Caravaggio is taken . . . also a Vergine of Masaccio."

"True," nodded Renato. With another lightning change of
expression, his eyes were tragic and soulful now. "They are
gone, lost. Beh, in the last years, a Crocefissione of Filippo Lippi,
a Carpaccio, a Trittico of Mantegna." His hands expressed delicately the enormity of the loss.

"There was a Bellini stolen last year in Rome," put in Marjorie
Bennett.

"That's a lovely Bellini Dr. Mowbray has." It was Doris's
tangential interruption. She threw a superior look at Beverley
as she spoke. "Her eyes are full of tragic mystery and compassion. You have a feeling of awe and reverence. It's really well
painted, too. Bambino looks as though he's jumping out of the
frame, really."

Beverley laughed, audibly. Her laugh had a touch of hysteria.
She drained her glass of wine. Lady Loftus exchanged a look
with Marjorie Bennett.

"I say," whispered Marjorie. "Is she, is Beverley . . ."

"Well, she was drunk back in Vicovaro," returned Lady Loftus shortly. "You won't find another word for it, Marjorie, no
matter how hard you try."

"She's quite young of course."

"Lack of moral fibre," said Lady Loftus decidedly.

"Of course," said Marjorie, "Beverley might have been born
here and educated in England, but she *is* an Australian."

"And what, Marjorie, has that to do with it?"

"Oh well, you know," said Marjorie Bennett, wriggling
slightly. "Anyway, she's not nearly so Australian now as she used
to be."

From the other side of the table, Doris's voice insisted. "I
bet," her flat little voice droned on, "Bellini's your favourite
painter now, isn't he, Dr. Mowbray? I had a peep once at that
Madonna you have in your study."

Doris shot a triumphant look at Beverley.

Mowbray laughed and looked ironically at Doris.

"I won't say you're wrong, Mrs. Boot. I am fond enough of
Bellini at least to have commissioned the excellent copy you
have seen, though it was more to help out a painter friend of

mine who was at the time very short of money. But as you say, this particular Madonna induces a feeling of . . . reverence. I say, do have some more wine, won't you?"

"I don't mind if I do," said Doris loudly, allowing Renato to fill her glass once more. She took a long draught. "Your painting isn't as pretty as some of his others, but that face fairly glows, doesn't it?" Doris fell into a reverie.

"Bellini puzzles me." Beverley spoke dreamily, though she enunciated impeccably. "His Madonnas are such a varied set. Some of them quite mystical, others very much flesh and blood. One of them reminds me of no one more than that vapid little TV announcer on Rete Due who comes on at around nine at night."

Mowbray nodded. "You're right. But then, he painted hundreds of women—"

"At least he could paint," Raffaella broke in vehemently. "They could all paint then—divinely. But no longer. Artists have lost the power . . ."

Juliette bristled.

"But no, not at all, it is not so!" she stammered. "Professor Mowbray, you cannot agree, after your lecture of two weeks ago. Art is the expression of our age, and our age is not of the fifteenth century. It is the age of the hydrogen bomb, of decadence, a lack of faith . . ."

"In the fifteenth century," Raffaella said scornfully, "no one painted badly. Painting was in the hands of masters. The artist began as an apprentice to a master. Nowadays, everyone will paint, and it accounts for the dreadful rubbish one sees any day in exhibitions—"

"So! It is so terrible, then, that people paint?" burst out Juliette. She spoke very seriously. "The dilettanti, as you call them. Assuredly I am one of them. I have not trained, except"—her voice became ironical—"for ten years only in my youth, when I attend an Academy of Art."

"For once Juliette isn't play-acting," thought Beverley.

Juliette spoke calmly now, but her eyes had filled with tears.

"I paint!—and you say I cannot. All right! But it allows me to enjoy all the more the work of those great artists who can." She turned defiantly to Raffaella. "Am I a criminal, Madame, be-

cause I have not devoted a lifetime to art? My painting, poor as
it is, in some measure replace the children I have never had, my
husband lost years ago. You will . . . No, no, this is enough!"
And the tears coursed down her cheeks.

"Oh Juliette," Beverley's voice sang down the scale, "Raffaella was not talking about *your* paintings. They are delightful.
Her standards are impossibly high. No doubt she would like to
stop all art immediately, by special order of the government."
Beverley giggled, dangerously.

Lady Loftus raised her voice at this point and proceeded
resolutely to talk Beverley down.

"We were talking of thefts of works of art," she said loudly and
irrelevantly. "I must say," she shot a severe look at Beverley, "I
would rather see anything stolen than a painting hanging in a
public gallery. So many people are thereby the losers."

But Beverley was not in a mood to submit and pounced with
lightning quickness.

"That's at least impersonal. Surely it's not as bad as stealing
from one person alone. Of course, there are many classes of
theft—so many different ways of robbing." She grasped a decanter, which in her slightly unsteady hand struck her wineglass
with a loud crystalline ring. "People steal paintings . . ." She
laughed again, turning now to Raffaella. "They also steal . . .
motor cars, silver spoons, children . . . even husbands."

She laughed again wildly and drained her glass. There was a
shocked silence. Raffaella cast an appalled glance at her, coloured deeply, and turned helplessly to Renato, who did not fail
her, but immediately poured words into the void—agitated,
meaningless words, which suddenly were lost in a shattering
blast from outside. For an instant the tall windows were gashes
of cruel quivering fire, and then, with the force of the gale
whistling through, the candles were extinguished, and there
remained blackness, the cries of the women and, dreadful to
hear, above all, the wailing of Lucia.

*"Santo Cielo! Dio ci manda la punizione dei nostri peccati. E
un presagio, come è' accaduto al imperatore Nerone . . ."**

---

* Nero had a grandiose villa near Subiaco (Sublaqueum in ancient times). At a
banquet in the villa the table before Nero was struck by lightning, which was
taken to be a portent of the end of his reign.

For some minutes confusion reigned, while peal upon peal of thunder burst upon the mountain. Then, realising—all of them —that the monastery held firm and that they were all in fact still alive, a torch was produced, a lantern lit and the resonant tones of Mowbray, cursing as he sought for more lights, were heard above the outburst of frightened voices.

"For heaven's sake, someone shut that blasted woman up. It's nothing. Only the storm."

Another enormous crash drew more screams from the women.

"By Jove, all hell's let loose tonight." Mowbray's tense face was eerily illumined as he lighted more candles.

Lucia's wails died down and the candle-light revealed her husband's arms clasped around her, rocking her to and fro. Mowbray glanced round at his party, some of whom had left the table and stood, comfortably close together, at the back of the hall.

"There's something at the door . . ." Juliette stammered. "Do you not hear . . . ?"

"She's right. It's a knocking on the door."

It was enough to set Lucia wailing once more in terror. Renato, with a half-fearful, half-scornful air, grasped a candle-stick and walked down the long hall towards the great oak door. He paused for an instant before drawing the bolt. An icy current drove into the hall and lightning outlined the dark figure on the threshold.

"*Un fantasmo!*" moaned Lucia. "The ghost of the emperor . . ."

The figure stepped slowly in and Renato fell back. It was no ghost however. It was John Backhouse.

VIII

The silence was complete. Then Renato fell back and stood gaping as Backhouse, blinking stupidly in the light of Renato's candelabrum, stumbled in, water dripping from his mackintosh.

Mowbray, the first to recover his poise, hastened forward. His exquisitely-spoken English, his half-bantering tone, fell soothingly on their ears.

"Good heavens! Backhouse! But damn it all, you're in Africa!"

John Backhouse shook his head, bringing down a shower of raindrops, and slowly removed his raincoat, before pulling a handkerchief from his pocket and dazedly rubbing it over his plastered wet hair.

"The storm caught me," he muttered. "I got in this morning earlier than I thought and felt like a jaunt."

No one chose to speak and the silence petrified them. Beverley had stayed frozen to her seat at the table, only her eyes following Backhouse's progress down the hall. She was very pale. He stopped by the table and said, "Beverley," in a strangely uncertain way, and getting no response took the seat by the fire that was offered him.

Van Dam, with a soundless laugh, poured whisky into a glass and Backhouse took it thankfully.

"I've been sitting in the car down there," he explained, "but it didn't look as though the rain would stop for hours."

"If you want to change your trousers, I have a spare pair," Van Dam offered pleasantly.

Mowbray, glancing at Beverley, gave an ironical smile when he noted she had still not made the slightest move to join her husband.

"You had better change right away, hadn't you?" said Van Dam. "My trousers will be too long, but I think we're much of a girth."

Suddenly Beverley rose with a funny little shake of her head and, pausing only to light a cigarette, tripped down the hall and stood before her husband.

"What a perfect miracle of timing! You rode the thunderbolt like Dr. Strangelove on his missile!" Her voice was full of laughter. "Lucia thought you were a ghost."

His face, into which some colour had crept and which had had a rough, stern, withdrawn look about it, seemed to disintegrate.

"I'll go and change," he said heavily. "Perhaps a shower."

"The bathroom's pretty rudimentary. "André'll show you, won't you, darling?" And Beverley turned on André an extravagant smile.

"And while you're changing, Raffaella will see about some dinner for you," added Mowbray, regarding his wife, who stood silently at the back of the group. His expression might easily have passed for unconcern. He turned back to Backhouse, with every appearance of goodwill. "We are to have a lecture later on. Will we be able to tempt you?"

"I feel rather dead-beat. I think I might turn straight into bed after a bite of food."

Backhouse drained his glass, keeping his eyes trained downwards and religiously in front of him as he rose and followed Van Dam out of the hall.

Coffee was served, and straight after Jo Ann's voice clattered in the vastness.

"Raffaella tells me they want us out for a little so the hall can be arranged for the lecture. I'll go get the lantern, girls, if you're ready, and I'd be happy if you'd all come and try a little glass of Sublacense to keep out the cold."

Mowbray raised his face from the slide projector as they made off.

"Lecture at nine-thirty," he called after them. "Augusto will ring the bell, remember, which you *should* hear in the cells."

He smiled to himself a little as they made their voluble way out.

John Backhouse, pushing open the door to the big hall a little later, almost walked straight into Raffaella. He stopped abruptly. She glanced back to the far side of the hall where

Mowbray was at work, his back to them, and stretched out her hands.

"*Why* have you come?" she breathed.

He did not answer, and his eyes were cold and hard as she had never before seen them, travelling slowly over her. His lips curled.

"All dressed up tonight—even ear-rings!"

Hatred distorted his face for an instant. He uttered one word and pushed her aside; then he walked with deliberate steps towards the fire, where Lucia, appearing from the back regions, accosted him.

"Your dinner is ready in the kitchen, Signore. There it is warm, if you do not mind to eat there."

She faltered at the look on his face. John Backhouse silently followed her from the hall.

The party repaired to the cells, Van Dam and Barbicinti to Mr. Tsuda's to share a bottle of Suntory Scotch, while Jo Ann entertained the ladies. Beverley and Hedda had disappeared.

"A *most* unfortunate occurrence. We must exercise tact."

In Jo Ann's cell, Lady Loftus declined a liqueur, though she could not quite bring herself to dissociate herself from the conversation.

"I suppose," Juliette, bothered by no such inhibitions and rather flushed of face, flopped untidily on to Jo Ann's bed, " 'E 'as come in secret to see his darling, his sweetheart Raffaella"— she gave absurd emphasis to the last syllable—"to surprise her for one moment only. To see how is she behaving in his absence." Juliette laughed strangely.

"Mowbray is as cool as a cucumber," put in Louise Parsons.

Lady Loftus sniffed. "He *is* a civilised being, Louise, and he *is* English."

"Waal, that's interesting," said Jo Ann. "I shouldn't have said he was so much at ease, the old prof. I was watching him pretty close, and I remember saying to myself, 'Well, brother, this time you're being extended to the limit and you're dealing with it real good.' But then," she continued ruminatively, "I kind of saw a little something in his face once or twice, back there in the hall, that was cold like steel."

Without warning, there intruded on the momentary silence a hollow, eerie music, without body or volume. It hung thin and shell-like above them, strange and awful in that utterly quiet place.

"*Mon-dieu!* It is ghost music." Juliette's eyes glittered in comic-dramatic fashion.

"Oh, it's the weekly pop-session!" exclaimed Louise suddenly. "Relayed by radio from Rome. *Canzonissima.* Surely you've heard it. Has someone got a transistor concealed about her?"

When they denied it, Louise insisted, "That's what it is. I recognise the theme song." She glanced at her watch. "Yes, it's just eight-thirty. It's just beginning."

Jo Ann poked her head out of the door. "Not a sound out there." She swung round suddenly. "Girls, it's the echo—that acoustical trick the prof. was telling about. Only he's put on a radio instead. Maybe he thought he'd take a rise out of us." She went out into the corridor, calling, "Come and check your own cells."

There was a rapid exit, and in a few minutes the efficacy of the rock-echo was established. The ladies returned to Jo Ann's cell to finish their liqueurs.

A few minutes later the eerie sound still assailed them when there was a knock at the door and Doris entered headlong, her eyes round and hard as buttons. She trembled with contained knowledge.

"If that's a drink," she breathed, "I could do with it."

With enjoyment, she took a glass and seated herself deliberately.

"Those two . . ." She waved a hand vaguely.

"The Backhouses?"

"I mean *Mowbray* and Raffaella. Going it properly, hammer and tongs."

Lady Loftus drew herself up.

"I really do not wish to hear more, Doris." Glancing round regally, she rose and opened the door.

They hardly noticed her. All eyes were firmly trained on Doris. Lady Loftus withdrew, though she omitted to close the door.

"I went out to get some drinking water from the kitchen,"

began Doris. "I thought the hall was empty and as I went through I thought I'd have a closer look at that lovely old screen of Mowbray's. I was right up to it when I realised those two were standing just the other side of it. They didn't hear me and no wonder."

"What do you mean?" Juliette hissed.

Screwing up her face, Doris sought to reproduce Mowbray's diction. " 'You may add to the general entertainment of my guests,' " she mimed, " 'but need you indulge them to this extent? We made a certain arrangement, you and I, that you and Backhouse would break with each other for three months. To-night he turns up here and before dinner I found you in Barbicinti's arms out there on the terrace. Could you possibly keep *control of your passions* for the next twenty-four hours?' Those were his very words!"

Doris sprang to her feet and drew herself up, assuming now a foreign inflection:

" 'You are vile, cruel. I did not ask John Backhouse to come here. As for Renato, I love him . . .' "

"Then Mowbray says: 'I find it hard to keep up with you. It was Backhouse only last month.' " Doris doubled up with laughter for a moment. " 'And,' he says, 'Barbicinti hasn't a penny.' "

"Then *she* says: 'Oh, he's made of flesh and blood, he's young and he loves me . . .' "

"An' Mowbray says: 'My dear girl, marry Barbicinti and you may find yourself even worse off . . .' "

"Then Raffaella says: 'Worse off! Could I be? Working like a slave for someone who no longer cares for me. How long now since every lira went on . . .' " Doris paused significantly, " 'on *her*—on that painted peasant of yours?' Those were her very words—'that painted peasant of yours.' "

"It doesn't sound like Mowbray," said Jo Ann.

"It's what she said. "An' then," Doris's eyes were round and awe-struck suddenly, " 'I'm leaving you and marrying Renato. I want a man, not a fanatic who cares for nothing but his books, his statues, his Bellini . . . Let me tell you that never again will that girl simper in front of me—never again!' "

"And then?" prompted Juliette, transfixed.

"Then," said Doris, "Mowbray said she'd better cool down. I

scuttled back to the kitchen for a while to let them get clear of the hall, and then I broke my neck getting back here."

"Mowbray and a peasant!" Jo Ann laughed a little uncomfortably.

Having heard their fill, they felt awkward and ashamed. Only Juliette, with an objective curiosity unhampered by scruple, said:

"Surely you have not heard it correctly, Doris. You have mixed it up."

"That I didn't!" Doris was defiant. "They were just the other side of the screen, and I heard every word."

"Were they shouting?"

"*No!* Mowbray was speaking very low and slow as you like. But every word cut like a knife." Doris suddenly subsided, worn out by excess of malice. "Ooh, I *have* got a headache. There's a good half-hour before the lecture starts. I must rest."

She went to the door. It was slightly ajar, as Lady Loftus had left it. Doris went out and pulled it shut behind her. As she did so, she was disconcerted to see Mowbray himself, his head bowed and his back to her, only a few feet away, bound no doubt for his own bedroom at the other end of the corridor.

IX

Summoned by the faint peals of a bell at nine-thirty, the little company made its way towards the big hall, shivering in the chilly air, the light evening-shoes of the ladies tapping incongruously on the stone slabs of the paving, candles flickering fitfully.

"Ah!" Juliette gave a throaty sigh of pleasure as they entered the hall. "It is as a theatre. Is it not really splendid?"

"It sure is, but it's also freezing cold down this end of the hall," complained Jo Ann. "Must we have that screen of Mowbray's between us and the fire?"

"Hush! It is to stop the light, so we see the picture better. Dr. Mowbray always has it thus," whispered Juliette reprovingly.

"Lord, what a draught from that door. Ah, that's better," sighed Jo Ann, as the last member of the class closed it.

Fumbling in the semi-darkness, they took their places on chairs facing the opposite wall. Mowbray stood at the back, and for the moment they were alone with the glowing scene projected onto the wall facing them—a lovely procession of early Quattrocento figures clustered in attitudes of reverence and joy, their robes falling in graceful folds from their firm and charming bodies. Little children clustered here and there at the knees of these glad, serene souls, and the whole gleamed with colours more enhanced than damaged by time.

"Lorenzo's 'Marriage of the Virgin.'" Hardly had the last member of his audience taken a seat than Mowbray had begun speaking, as usual abruptly claiming their attention. "This time from Santa Trinità in Florence. It forms part of the Story of the Virgin ordered by the Bankers' Guild, one of the most typical upper-middle-class corporations, about 1420.

"Why did they choose him? Mr. Tsuda has already raised this question. You will remember that Florence was still under the spell of the Gothic style, felt by the monastic world to be more reverent than the naturalistic art of a Masaccio . . ."

Mowbray had won the attention of them all. His powerful, resonant voice rang effortlessly and beautifully distinct through the vast hall, and not the least rustle of a skirt or squeak of a chair disturbed his delivery. They sat enthralled, with none of the questions and whispered asides which had at times disturbed the Rome lectures.

"Well, of course they chose him first of all because he was a painter of great quality, but also because Lorenzo is only half-way along the road towards the powerful modelling and strength which was the aim of a Masaccio. We'll have, by way of contrast, a Madonna and Child by Masaccio, please Raffaella. Ah yes. How lovely she is, isn't she, with her simple lines and attitude, that eternal, resigned look of care and attention. She is half-resting, but ever watchful. We'll have the 'Nativity of the Virgin' now, if you please, Raffaella. Thank you. Now, as I was saying . . . What's that, Raffaella? Oh yes rather, of course, my dear. I'll see you out. Take this torch with you and go off and rest."

From behind the audience came the sound of footsteps and the mutter of voices. The door opened and closed, sending an icy current of air around their legs.

"My wife is not feeling well and needs to return to her room. You'll excuse me if I take just a little more time to work the projector also. As I was saying," Mowbray continued easily, "a painter such as Lorenzo . . ."

He paused as the door opened once more, and there was a slight groan from the ladies as the draught whipped their legs again when the door closed, and round the side of the screen a slim figure appeared quietly and after some whispering took her place on the remaining empty chair.

"I had really thought we were all assembled," Mowbray said, his voice betraying extreme testiness. "If you are quite settled now, Mrs. Boot, we will proceed."

"Can't always help being late, can you," said Doris to Juliette, who was next to her.

"He gathers speed now," whispered Juliette in return. "He could so easily lose the thread of what he says . . ."

"Given the enormous religious impulses of the age," went on Mowbray, enunciating each word clearly and pointedly as though to defy anyone to talk further, "we can see how the style of a Lorenzo might please . . ."

Fresco after fresco of Spinello, of Lorenzo, trembled, moved and stayed glowingly at rest on the great screen of the opposite wall, to the accompaniment of Mowbray's glittering commentary.

"We will now turn," he said, "to the great revolutionary in painting, Giotto. He died in 1337, thirty-four years before Lorenzo was even born. Doesn't it seem strange that the one—so much more startlingly dramatic a painter, who saw life in the round and gave it such warmth in his painting—should have preceded the other by something like a hundred years?

"Just look at Giotto's 'Lamentation over the Body of the Dead Christ' from the chapel of the Scrovegni in Padova. Giotto has created the sacred story in paint before our very eyes. Foreshortening, modelling, deep shadows—nothing like this had been done for a thousand years . . ."

Had Doris dropped off to sleep, bemused with food and too

much wine? Beside her Juliette's beautiful face was faintly visible in the glow from the screen, her brilliant eyes shining with sympathy and enthusiasm. What was Mowbray talking about?

Doris felt uncomfortable, and wished it was all over. The fire and vigour of Mowbray's discourse raised no chord in her, and she was barely conscious that he was finishing his lecture. He was speaking of artists as the most valuable members of any community.

". . . Imagine a world without *Hamlet,* without *Lear,* without those gravely cheerful, gloriously human churches of the Florentine Renaissance. So, you are resting, Madame?"

Doris awoke with a great start, jolted by Juliette. Someone had uttered something between a loud grunt and a snore. Could it have been Doris herself? Mowbray's words, his shaming words, rang in her ears. A little ripple of laughter ran round the hall.

"And yet you should not!" Mowbray's voice thundered out menacingly. He was the actor now, the rapt audience held in an iron vice. "You should not be. Have you ever wondered, Madame, just how much we owe to artists—artists of all sorts? Imagine history without the help of painting, of sculpture, of literature. What would we know of how people lived, thought, spoke, ate, dressed? How barren a picture we would have. We would have nothing to cling to. But how much more than that have artists done for us . . ."

Even now Doris did not take it in at all. And how could she? Since, as Juliette whispered, she had been dozing for the last hour.

". . . and you might almost say that without art there would be no real communication among men and you would live in a world ugly and inconceivable."

Mowbray's voice died away. The lecture was finished. His voice had faltered slightly on the last words and his audience stayed silent for a moment before a murmur of applause rose.

It was no time, they felt, for vulgar exclamations of thanks. The lecture had been unique. Doris alone sat stolid and unyielding. Even Jo Ann, though afterwards only able to describe the lecture as "a wow," knew that it had been something more than she might reasonably have expected in return for the handsome number of dollars she had expended.

They found their voices at last, however, and Mowbray took the place of honour near the fire, while Lucia carried in candles and Augusto brought a great jug of coffee. Jo Ann, with a laugh, produced a second bottle of Benedictine liqueur. The party relaxed joyfully.

"What a performance!" exclaimed Juliette. "I can tell you, my dears, I have listened many times over the years to lectures of this sort, and never do I hear this quality before. And never a note, never a piece of paper. It wells up, so . . ." She drank, and gestured freely towards the ceiling. Looking across to where Mowbray was deep in conversation with Renato Barbicinti, she continued. "And he does not appear in the least tired. He gathers more strength as he proceeds. What a fount of information is there, only to be tapped. A pity he is old and will finally die," she added quaintly.

"Beverley is not with us," commented Lady Loftus, gazing at two coffee cups as yet untouched. "Nor Hedda."

"To have missed this, poor Beverley. Why?" Juliette, flushed, her eyes glittering with excitement, was all concern.

Doris sniffed.

"Beverley had had a lot to drink."

"She wasn't the only one, Doris," commented Lady Loftus severely.

"Have a look at this." Jo Ann held out a hand in the palm of which sparkled a bright blue stone. "Sapphire, isn't it? I just found it on the floor over there."

"It is so. And it is from the ear-ring of Raffaella Mowbray surely."

"I had better give the stone to him, then."

Jo Ann hesitated, gazing over to where Mowbray still talked to Renato.

"Yes, well, I shan't interrupt them," she said shortly. "I for one am for bed." She yawned. "What a day. The stone will keep until tomorrow."

"I'll come with you," Doris offered. "It's just on twelve-thirty."

"I wish to put a small question to Dr. Mowbray." Juliette floated away, waving her cigarette holder.

"How the old boy keeps it up," commented Doris to Jo Ann, as the two women, shivering in the sudden chill of the corridor, directed their steps to the cells.

"He's getting very profound," returned Jo Ann. "Whoever realised there was so much in all this art stuff? Of course, you couldn't take a single note in the dark. I'm doing another course of lectures just now, on Russian art, and I get a bit mixed up between the two. What I always say, though, is that something sticks."

Pausing before the door marked "Signora Mowbray," Jo Ann tapped on it lightly.

"I don't suppose she'd still be awake."

Cautiously she pushed open the door and poked her head in.

"Bed's empty," she said, squinting in the light of her candle. "Still made up." She shut the door. "I'll keep the sapphire till morning."

"Well." An expression of quiet satisfaction, unpleasant to observe, came over Doris's face. "If she's not sleeping in her own bed, you can hardly go seeking her out, can you?"

Jo Ann looked at her for a second, and burst out laughing.

"You're right," she chuckled. "I hardly think I can."

This set them off laughing again, all down the corridor.

Back in the big hall, the little nucleus remained around Mowbray, while there developed between him, Mr. Tsuda and Renato Barbicinti a free-ranging discussion of the role of the artist in society, the concept being tossed backwards and forwards like a bright glittering ball, intercepted occasionally by Juliette, who hovered eager, breathless, throaty at their side, to be snatched with maddening swiftness once more from her grasp, while Van Dam, well out of his depth, was barely allowed to do more than brush against it, before it was swept once more from his disparaging hands, and Lady Loftus, Mrs. Bennett, Mrs. Parsons gazed and listened, awestruck and mystified, as from a safe distance.

It was, as Juliette was later to tell the others, a dialogue such as was only rarely and by the merest chance heard in these days of much chatter and scant conversation, conducted moreover by men who were artists and creators themselves in the depth and strength of their appreciation, men of the finest perceptions and most exquisite intelligence, in this exciting if restricted avenue—in short, brilliant theorists and critics, *la crème de la crème.*

They drank more wine, while they talked, and Lucia and Augusto, having thrown yet more logs on the fire, retired at last. Outside, without anyone noticing, the storm died, and the moon, appearing dramatically from behind black massed clouds, sailed serenely across a clear, newly washed sky.

Leading Lady

X

"It is a choir of angels."

Juliette, just after nine o'clock the following morning, stood on the outside terrace of San Donato, regarding the golden brilliance of the sun which burst in curiously symmetrical rays from behind a bank of dark clouds. She addressed the words to Renato, interrupting his nervous pacing up and down.

"It is, after all, the land of Bernini," he shrugged. "It is theatrical in the best Baroque tradition." He stretched and shook his curly locks. "Poetry before breakfast is not in order. I shall wait until after my coffee to admire the beauty of the morning."

Juliette flushed.

"Do what you want. It is entirely your privilege."

She turned her back on him and swept inside, and Renato followed her at a distance to the refectory table where he gulped down a cup of black coffee.

"He fidgets and worries and he will soon lose his temper," pronounced Juliette, into the ready ear of Doris, who slid into a chair beside her. "His darling," her lips curled, "he cannot find and he dare not ask for her."

"His darling," muttered Doris, "didn't sleep in her bed last night."

"What!" Juliette was scathing. "In the presence of her husband, in this place of abstinence and self-denial!"

"Well," said Doris impassively. "Jo Ann just checked. It looks as though her bed wasn't slept in all night."

"So." Juliette was incredulous.

Through the door from the terrace Jo Ann burst in, Louise Parsons on her heels.

"We shan't get away this morning," she called.

"Why?"

"There's been a landslide. About a kilometre or so down the road there. Looks as though half the mountain had come down." Jo Ann plumped down into a chair near Juliette and heaved a sigh of exhaustion. "We walked down and there it was."

"What!" Juliette jumped up, her hand on her heart.

"We met Augusto and he says the telephone is still operating," explained Jo Ann. "He expects them to send men and equipment up, but you know how slowly things can move here. It's Sunday, too."

"*When* did this happen?" Juliette stuck her face almost into Jo Ann's. Her over-reaction might have been due to Jo Ann's heartiness, hard to bear this early in the morning.

"It must have been very recent—last couple of hours or so—because Mr. Tsuda's car got away all right."

"So." Juliette subsided once more.

"Here is Dr. Mowbray," said Lady Loftus coolly. She looked exasperated with Latin dramatics. "How tired he looks this morning."

"We saw Mr. Backhouse outside—all alone," commented Jo Ann, her voice only slightly less sonorous than usual. "My, how hung-over he looked."

"He didn't want to speak to us, that was clear," piped up Louise. "He took one look and turned on his heel."

"*Mon Dieu!*" Juliette's hand flew to her mouth and the others saw her eyes were on Beverley, who entered just then, closely followed by Van Dam.

"What's the matter?" enquired Jo Ann.

"Beverley . . ." Juliette stammered. "How white she is." She rose once more and walked towards the newcomers.

"My dear. We are having coffee. Won't you sit down?"

Beverley shot a vaguely surprised look at her, and slid into a chair, lighting a cigarette. She looked, not eighteen this morning, but all of her twenty-eight years.

Van Dam looked dreadful. He stared hard at Juliette as though she offended his eyes, then turned away to pour coffee for himself. Then he sat down beside Jo Ann.

"Pace too much for me, Jo Ann." His face was pasty and grim. "You're a stouter soul than I am. Those Martinis, and all the rest."

"Mr. Tsuda left early, just the same." Juliette's voice was loud, nervous and insistent. "Before the landslide. *He* was lucky."

Van Dam looked over at her morosely.

"You know of the landslide?" Juliette demanded of Van Dam.

"I know about the landslide," he grunted.

"It did not stop Tsuda getting away," Juliette repeated nervously.

Van Dam winced. "So you already said." He spoke with insolent deliberation. "Tsuda has a head like iron, it seems."

"Barbicinti doesn't seem to have suffered," observed Jo Ann.

"Oh, he's Italian, and they don't drink." Van Dam gulped down some coffee and grimaced.

Hedda, entering with Lucia, went up to Dr. Mowbray.

"Lucia is wondering if she should make up the beds again. It doesn't seem we will get away today."

"We can only wait and see." Mowbray knit his brows, and turned to Lucia. "You'd better do the rooms at once," he said in Italian. "We're all out now, aren't we?" He glanced round the hall.

"Your wife isn't." Jo Ann glanced expressively at Doris.

"Go and wake my wife," Mowbray instructed Lucia, "and then get on with the beds."

"Nice to see the sun again," commented Doris, as Lucia departed. "It's a different place this morning."

"Of course," Juliette looked nervously at the others, "there is lacking the atmosphere of last night. The candle-light is missing, the storm, the conversation about the table, the *esprit.*" Getting no response, she faltered. "We have all too much drunk and this morning feel the effects," she ended, rather naïvely.

"You can say that again," rejoined Jo Ann rather tartly.

"In vino veritas," Doris grimaced.

Juliette gazed absently at her for a second, then swept on nervously.

"The mystery of this hall last night, with the table a pool of light in the centre and the blackness of the surroundings. It was so beautiful, exactly like a stage-play." She laughed, self-consciously. "And we the actors."

"That woman really *is* a little crazy," Jo Ann muttered to Louise Parsons.

There was a commotion at the other end of the table prompted by the reappearance of Lucia.

"The *signora*, she is nowhere to be found!" she exclaimed.

"What?" Mowbray rose to his feet, his face creased with sudden anxiety. "What do you mean?"

"The bedrooms are empty, Professore, also the bathroom."

"She must be out walking, then."

"She could be looking at the frescoes." Renato jumped up. "I'll see." He hurried from the hall.

"Has anyone seen her this morning?" enquired Mowbray.

"She wasn't in her room last night when I looked in." Jo Ann spoke slowly. "Or this morning." She took a screwed-up piece of paper from her pocket and handed it to Mowbray. "I wanted to return the stone out of her ear-ring. I found it on the floor over there last night."

Renato burst into the hall, nearly knocking over Augusto, who had been hovering just inside the door. "She's not downstairs. We must search outside."

Marjorie Bennett had finished her coffee and strolled out on the terrace a moment or two before. She now re-entered the hall almost on the steps of Renato. The only one of the party who was rarely heard to utter a word, sheltering habitually as she did in the shadow cast by Lady Loftus, she made now her one important pronouncement of the day.

"Out there on the . . . I looked over the wall," she stammered. "There's something down there. There's—" Her pretty matronly face blanched and, putting a hand to her mouth, she collapsed on the nearest chair.

Renato had turned and raced out through the door. The others, hurrying out after him, lined the terrace wall on either side of him.

"Yes . . ." said Renato, his voice hardly audible. "Yes—" He gave a sob, and clapped his hands to his head. Over everything there suddenly sounded a high scream from one of the women, a kind of braying, "No, no, no . . ." The noise went on and on.

"She's a long way down." Jo Ann's voice trembled violently. "Oh my God, she's a long way down."

Van Dam, with a sweeping motion of his powerful arms, pushed two of the women aside and looked over the edge. He muttered something, then swung round as Mowbray, deathly white in the face, spoke behind him.

"Let me through."

In his turn, Mowbray set his hands on the balustrade, a hoarse sound breaking from him at the sight of the splodge of black velvet, an out-thrust arm, the only two components distinguishable of the grotesquely doubled-up form which lay on an outcrop of rock some eighty or a hundred metres below.

For what seemed minutes Mowbray remained immobile with bowed head. Then he slowly turned. His mouth opened, but for a time he could get nothing out. Then he swallowed and at last managed:

"Get her up."

Renato took him by the arm.

"*Coraggio.* We must be calm." He spoke in Italian, his voice thick with emotion, mocking his words. "Professor Mowbray, I beg you, come inside. She is . . . past help, I think."

The two disappeared inside.

Van Dam said savagely, swinging after them:

"Where's that man—Augusto? Go and find him." He rapped the words out and Mrs. Bennett, who happened to be in front of him, sped off.

When Augusto appeared, his eyes filled with tears at the sight below.

"*Dio mio. La povera bella signora.*"

"It's a sheer drop from here. Is there another way down?" snapped Van Dam.

"There is another way," replied Augusto, his face working. "Come." He turned and led Van Dam down the steps to the lower terrace. Barbicinti, rushing out distractedly at that moment, followed them.

"Rope. We need rope." Renato was grotesque in his impatience.

"There is rope," replied Augusto. "Plenty of rope from the *lavori* . . . To get her up is not possible. From down there, if we can secure her with ropes, she could be lowered down the rock face to a place I know of. From there she could be brought up. Except"—his face worked—"she will bump against the rock. She will be—"

"She's dead, you fool," Renato sobbed. "Can't you see she's dead?"

Augusto gave him a compassionate look and said:

"I go now to fetch rope."

He was back very soon, a long length of rope coiled round his waist, another length over his arm. Expertly, he knotted a length round a pillar of the balustrade and threw it over. "It will serve," he said, looking down. "There is enough, and to spare."

He turned to Van Dam.

"You also will come."

"I am certainly coming," said Renato violently. He measured up to Augusto.

"Yes, yes, Signore." Augusto did not argue.

In silence, the group on the upper terrace watched the three men make their way down.

"I go inside. This I cannot support." Juliette, her face flooded with dangerous colour, walked shakily into the big hall. "It is too horrible. How long since . . . How long?"

"She didn't—" Doris began her refrain.

"We know she didn't sleep in her bed last night!" Juliette cried hoarsely. "But God, can she have been there all night?"

"I'd say so."

"Dr. Mowbray. Look at him. It is awful to watch. Have you ever seen a face like that? He has not spoken. He will not speak . . ."

Juliette burst into tears.

Out on the terrace, Beverley had stood watching the men go down. She was quite still, her two hands ranged neatly together on the parapet, her face expressionless.

To the women inside the big hall, to the others outside, an interminable time seemed to pass.

"I cannot . . . no, I cannot go out." Juliette shivered at certain noises from outside, finally. Doris suddenly rose and disappeared.

"It's all right. There are plenty to help." Lady Loftus, who had joined Juliette, spoke gently.

"I am a coward." Juliette stammered.

"There are plenty to help," repeated Lady Loftus.

"They will take her to the cell, no?"

The futile exchange of words went on. It seemed hours before Doris came back, Van Dam following.

"Have you brought her up?" Lady Loftus's voice was sharp with tension.

"No, we didn't bring her up," he said harshly.

"It was too difficult?"

"Don't know about that." It was Doris who spoke now.

"She is . . ."

"She's dead. She's been dead for hours," Doris said.

Van Dam turned on his heel and went over to the table by the fire, where he poured himself a drink.

"How could she fall? It is incredible," Juliette faltered.

"It's a rather low balustrade. But it is incredible, all the same," agreed Lady Loftus. "And not a soul to see it."

"Someone saw it all right," said Doris quietly.

"Who was it?" cried Lady Loftus.

"That we don't know," Doris stated solemnly. "But whoever it was put a bullet into her before she went over."

"No, you're crazy." Juliette clapped a hand to her mouth and Lady Loftus gave a cry.

"She was shot," insisted Doris shortly. She looked at them calmly for a moment before she added, "So of course we can't touch her." She lowered her voice. "The police wouldn't like it. And anyway, it would be a job, because . . ." Her voice died.

"What do you mean?"

"I mean, because of the state she's in," said Doris doggedly, her little eyes darting from face to face. "After that fall, and then out all night in that weather—"

"Don't, stop it!" Lady Loftus's hand went to her mouth. "Doris, you can't mean it! Are you really saying she was shot before she went over?"

"Can't have been after she went over, can it?" said Doris reasonably.

There was complete silence while the others filed inside.

"I fear for Dr. Mowbray. At his age . . ." Lady Loftus shuddered.

"Renato Barbicinti is with him," said Doris.

"Renato is not in much better state by the look of him. Oh," Lady Loftus gasped suddenly. "Mr Backhouse! Hadn't someone better look for Mr. Backhouse?"

She stopped in confusion as Mowbray and Barbicinti entered the hall. At the same time Van Dam strode over to join them.

Mowbray's face was ashen and he spoke slowly and mechanically.

"You all know what has happened." His voice faltered.

Van Dam interrupted him, taking charge almost angrily.

"Professor Mowbray wishes to inform you that his wife died— we think some hours ago—as the result of a bullet wound. How she came to fall over the balcony we do not know. We did not find a weapon. Signor Barbicinti has been in touch with the police in Subiaco. There is no possibility of anyone coming immediately as we are completely blocked off up here. Nothing has been done about the landslide, though the police hope that work will begin this afternoon to clear the road. In the meantime—"

Renato broke in, his voice only just under control.

"Raffaella was shot. The police—they've given instructions that we touch nothing and remain here—just as if . . ."

"Just as if," Beverley laughed mirthlessly, "we could do anything else."

Several heads turned towards her, and Lady Loftus hastily said, sounding rather uncertain:

"It is absurd, of course, that anyone here should be suspected of . . . of . . ."

"Lady Loftus!" Renato's voice trembled. "We are *all* under suspicion."

The door to the terrace was suddenly pushed open. Renato swung round and cried, *"Santo cielo!* Signor Backhouse . . ."

John Backhouse, his face ashen, stood on the threshold once more, this time bright sunlight outlining a dishevelled figure, unshaven, without tie, and wearing Van Dam's ill-fitting trousers.

"I've been walking." His voice was quiet.

"Then you don't . . . you haven't heard . . ."

Backhouse's eyes travelled wearily round the group.

"Mrs. Mowbray is dead," said Van Dam quietly. "Her body has just been found down on a ledge under the terrace there."

John's eyes sought Beverley's face.

"She is dead," he repeated, without surprise or emotion.

"She was shot," rapped out Renato. "Through the head. Whoever shot her then pushed her over."

"Shot." John Backhouse repeated the word even as—unwittingly theatrical—he clapped a hand to his head and staggered forward.

"Quickly! Catch him."

"John!" Beverley's cry rang out as she ran to him, but André Van Dam had caught him as he fell.

"Sit him down and put his head between his knees," ordered Jo Ann. "He has fainted. That's all." She turned round. "Beverley!"

But Beverley had rushed forward to support her husband, and the others saw that tears were streaming down her face.

XI

All morning they hung about in little groups, disbelief struggling with growing acceptance. They kept together in the big hall. Outside was horror, possibly danger. Mowbray had been helped to his cell and had not reappeared.

Van Dam strode round restlessly, grim and pale, occasionally sneezing and blowing his nose. Lady Loftus, not for nothing the doyenne of the Consortium wives, presided over a little circle formed by Marjorie Bennett, Jo Ann Partridge, Louise Parsons and Doris Boot, grave but also incredulous that violence should have impinged on their uneventful lives. Juliette, adding drama to drama, worked off her nervousness by sheer floods of talk—to Barbicinti when he chose to come near her, to Beverley, who remained speechless beside Hedda, to André Van Dam. Augusto had gone down once more on the rope, taking with him a large rug to cover the body. It was, for the time being, all he could do.

At eleven Lucia, acting under Lady Loftus's instructions, carried in coffee and they gathered round the table.

"Oh Mr. Backhouse, this is awful, awful!" Marjorie Bennett turned to John Backhouse with a little moan.

But John Backhouse only muttered, "Dreadful, yes of course." And turned away, to continue his restless pacing up and down, always absorbed in his own thoughts.

"I feel sure it was a terrible accident. The poor gel was dreadfully upset yesterday after the wheel came loose on her Simca and probably had all sorts of fears. If she had been carrying a gun as some sort of protection against these imaginary dangers, well, it isn't uncommon for guns to go off." Lady Loftus's words fell loud and clear. Was this a rehearsal of the line she would take with the police later on? Her eyes skimmed the others, resting no longer or more meaningfully on Beverley than on anyone else.

"Sometimes," Jo Ann's voice held a hint of eagerness, "I hear those hunters popping away at daybreak and I think I wouldn't like to be out and about near them. What if poor Signora Mowbray simply got a stray bullet? I mean," her voice tailed off uncertainly, "if she had gone out very early . . ."

"On the side of a ravine, of course!" Renato's voice was scornful, with a hint of hysteria. He took from his pocket a small metal cylinder and held it out. "I suppose you realise what this is."

Van Dam, leaning over Renato's shoulder, uttered an exclamation.

"The cartridge case, eh? Wherever did you find that?"

"On the terrace, just outside the main door."

Van Dam sought out Beverley with his eyes. She turned away.

"If she took her own life," Van Dam began, and his eyes did not leave Beverley, "and the gun went over with her, it might never—"

"And why should she take her own life? She, who had everything to live for?" Renato's voice rose dangerously. His eyes flickered from Van Dam to Beverley.

"When did it happen?" Jo Ann asked. "Can anyone tell that?"

"She didn't sleep in her bed last night," offered Doris once again.

"There is one question we must ask." Van Dam's normally confident tones betrayed signs of strain.

"And what is this?" Juliette asked.

Van Dam looked round. No one moved.

"Who was carrying a gun?"

No one answered.

"I saw one last night," Van Dam went on grimly. "In fact, I pointed it out to Backhouse."

"You saw one?" Lady Loftus looked at Van Dam fearfully.

"On the window-ledge in the corridor, outside the cells."

"Indeed!" Lady Loftus made a movement of revulsion, her eyes downcast.

"Backhouse will tell you I saw it," Van Dam insisted. He looked straight at Beverley. "Later on the gun disappeared. It was gone by the time we went to bed."

Lady Loftus was flustered. "Mr. Backhouse . . ." She turned round as if to seek help.

But John Backhouse was no longer in the big hall.

"Oh, where is Mr. Backhouse?" Lady Loftus turned to Augustus, who hovered on the outskirts of the group.

"*Il Signor Backhouse è uscito, Signora.* He has gone outside, just a moment or so ago."

"Then please fetch him. Wait, Augusto, I will come with you." Together, they left the hall.

"We don't know how long we'll be holed up here without police protection." Van Dam's eyes roamed round the others. "Signora Mowbray was certainly killed by . . ." He paused, his eyes jerking to Beverley and away again.

"By one of us," supplied Jo Ann bluntly.

"Exactly so. And that person," Van Dam went on, "would have got rid of the gun."

"Oh yes," Renato said scornfully. "You may be sure the gun is safely at the bottom of the Aniene by now." His lips quivered.

"One of us!" Juliette gasped. Her face contorted, she clutched a chair for support. "Is this nightmare never to end?"

"It is so surprising, then?" demanded Renato. "You have forgotten the accident to her car? That an attempt on her life had already been made?"

"Of course it is incredible," said Van Dam, "that anyone should have done either. One is beginning to wonder if one of our number is not mentally deranged. Until the police arrive we would all do well to stay on the alert."

With a further grim look in Beverley's direction he turned and followed Lady Loftus and Augusto outside.

By the fireplace, Beverley and Hedda sat side by side without speaking. They both smoked an unaccustomed number of cigarettes. Hedda's hand just touched Beverley's, as it rested on the sofa seat.

"You did take my gun, Heddy," Beverley breathed. "Didn't you?"

Hedda's eyes assented, passing lovingly over the other girl's face.

"Did you loosen the wheel on her Simca?" whispered Beverley.

Hedda's hand closed over hers, unclenching Beverley's fingers one by one, gently rubbing her palm. Beverley coloured and gave a sob. Hedda, searching her face, saw terror in it.

Suddenly, with one accord, they turned their heads, aware that silence had fallen on the big hall. Mowbray was at the door, and the rest went towards him sympathetically. He bent an ear to Juliette, as Hedda and Beverley joined the group.

"You are very good." He had taken a seat and accepted coffee. His eyes, always striking, gazed blackly from a face showing now more than his age, a face deathly pale. "Raffaella was shot," he said, almost wonderingly.

Doris, who stood near him, said in her flat tones:

"It's been suggested . . . I mean, no one here could possibly have wanted to hurt your wife, not unless that person was out of his mind. And that's what we are thinking now . . ."

Mowbray suddenly got to his feet.

"I must get some air," he said.

"Then I shall go with you," Juliette said quickly.

"I could do with some fresh air myself," said Jo Ann abruptly. "Why don't we all go out?"

They went down the steps into the keen damp air of midday, down the newly flagstoned path, down the steep winding stair to the terrace on the lower level.

"Oh, there's Mr. Backhouse," commented Jo Ann, gesturing towards the figures standing round the boot of an open car. As they approached, however, the immobility of those round the car struck them. They stood without speaking, Augusto, Van Dam and Lady Loftus, gazing at John Backhouse, and he at them. Nor did they pay the slightest attention to the others until the latter were upon them. Then Jo Ann resolutely broke the silence.

"Has something happened?"

Lady Loftus, whose back had been half-turned to the newcomers, swung around with a little whimper, her hands seeming to deny the words of Augusto, who spoke hoarsely in Italian.

"La pistola . . . l'abbiamo trovata, la pistola, proprio qui." He indicated the open luggage compartment of the BMW, then bent down and turned up a plastic cover over the spare tyre. "Here under the spare tyre . . . is the gun."

Augusto's words died away in the still air and there was total silence for a long moment. Then two things happened. Renato, the gravel crunching under his feet, walked round the others to where John Backhouse stood, one hand on his own car. Confronting him, Renato's whole person spelt accusation and repulsion. And Lady Loftus was heard to say despairingly:

"I am quite sure there is some dreadful mistake. Mr. Backhouse, we appeal to you for help."

John Backhouse gave a short, mirthless laugh.

"For *help*, Lady Loftus?"

His eyes left her and were forced back to Renato.

"Signor Backhouse." Renato's tone was dangerous. "You are the owner of this gun?"

Backhouse said nothing. Renato turned to Van Dam.

"Is this the one you saw?"

Van Dam peered into the boot and said:

"It looks like it. A Walther. I saw it last night only by the light of a hurricane lamp."

"You haven't touched it, any of you?" Renato asked. "Augusto?"

The man shook his head and muttered something in rapid Italian to Renato.

John Backhouse laughed shortly.

"You needn't worry. The police perform miracles of detection nowadays when it's a case of firearms. You have only to wait."

"We will, naturally, wait." Renato's voice was dangerously calm. "We will wait." He breathed hard. "But now, we wait for your explanation, Signore. Augusto tells me you were seen by him and Lady Loftus to insert the key in this luggage compartment of your car, to open it, and to bring something out—this gun. And then they come to you. You stop. You replace the gun—"

"And I'm caught practically red-handed, is what you mean." Backhouse's voice was cold and almost detached. He looked down at Renato almost with indifference, his eyes flat, guarded.

"You are making a confession?" Renato's voice was suddenly thick and his voice stumbled over the words. "You have killed—"

"A confession!" Backhouse cut him off loudly and angrily. "I was opening the boot of my own car when Lady Loftus and the servant chap came up. Damn it, they saw me. There's no confession about it."

"A woman has died," cried Renato wildly, "killed with this gun. We demand an explanation."

"Demand away," returned Backhouse contemptuously. "You won't get it."

"Why . . ." Renato spluttered. "It is intolerable, not possible." He broke into Italian, turning to the others. "I call on you all for help!"

"And yet," said Backhouse, "you must nevertheless accept the fact that I have not the slightest intention of saying a word more."

"Why, you will—" Renato, a much smaller man, yet muscular, sprang at Backhouse suddenly, with a sob of rage. Backhouse pushed him away without effort.

"Try and calm down," he advised Renato. "Short of locking me up or putting handcuffs on me, neither of which is feasible, there's not much you can do until the police arrive. I am sure you feel like lynching me on the spot. But you have the keys of my car. The gun you may therefore keep safely out of further harm's way."

With a considerable degree of dignity, Backhouse turned his back on Barbicinti, threaded his way through the bystanders and sought out Beverley, who stood small and pale-faced on the other side of the BMW. He said something to her in a low voice and together they turned and walked slowly off down the hill.

Renato made a movement to follow, but Van Dam clapped a big hand on his shoulder.

"Leave him," he commanded roughly. "Leave him to his wife."

Once round a turning in the road and out of sight of the others, John grasped Beverley by the arm and swung her round to face him.

"We've got to talk. There's not much time."

She squirmed away, breathing hard.

"Now!" His voice was urgent. "I want the whole story."

She gave a cry.

"The whole story! Of what?"

"Stop that, for God's sake. Who else knows you brought that gun up here?"

She made no reply and he said impatiently:

"You know, don't you, the police can trace the ownership of the gun to us?"

Her eyes widened, and she gave a long, faltering sigh. "The police . . ."

"To you, more precisely. The gun is registered in your name. Had you forgotten?"

"Does that worry you?" Her voice was bitter. "You don't feel protective of *me*? At this late stage!"

"Don't laugh at me, Beverley." Backhouse's voice was heavy. "I want the truth."

Beverley stiffened, and her mouth opened. No words came.

"I was checking whether the gun was in the drawer, when I found the picture," snapped Backhouse.

Beverley laughed wildly, throwing back her head. "I see. Oh, I see. And you say that's why you came up here!"

His lips tightened.

"We've so little time," he said again. "Can't we deal with first things first? Who knew you carried a gun with you on this trip?"

She said nothing, her eyes wandering from him.

"Beverley," he pleaded. "You're in such danger. Surely you can try and be sensible now."

He attempted to put an arm round her shoulders, but she jerked away.

"So *I*'m in danger." She laughed, though there was fear in her eyes. She slumped back against the bole of an oak. "I'm in danger." Suddenly her voice was thick with sobs. "But *she's* dead. She's *dead*. She'll never hurt me again. She—and you!"

And she burst into tears.

"For Christ's sake." John's face darkened and he clenched and unclenched his hands, standing there looking down at her. "We've both got to tell the same story," he insisted, his voice controlling panic. "Can't you see that? Why the devil do you think I was stalling, back at the car?"

His words were lost, suddenly swallowed up by a staccato, juddering, monstrous onslaught of noise, and Beverley saw him standing there, his eyes full of pleading, his mouth opening and shutting, until he too submitted. A vast shadow passed over them, lifted, moved on. Beverley looked up fearfully at the ungainly vehicle with its madly spinning propellers. It circled, and again lumbered into position over their heads, now so close that faces could be seen peering out.

"They're coming in to land here where it's flat." John gripped Beverley's arm and forced her to run with him. The monster, with a juddering roar, tilted and prepared to begin its descent.

"It will be supplies," gasped Beverley.

"Supplies! It's a *Carabinieri* helicopter and it'll be full of police. Do you believe now that we haven't much time?"

In the Wings

XII

"So no one saw her after she left the lecture last night about ten and went off to bed with a headache."

Commissario Gadda looked up from his sergeant's already copious notes. He had a broad pale face framed in close-cut, light brown hair growing low down temples and cheeks. His skin was pasty and imperfect and looked grubby.

"What time did the Japanese leave?"

"No one actually saw him go. About five a.m. they think."

Gadda consulted a report and read: "Entrance wound in left temple, exit wound on level with and five centimetres to left of occiput. No powder markings. Weapon definitely fired beyond range of self-infliction. The gun is bound to be the Backhouse Walther, but it's got to be tested."

"Does the doctor know when she was killed?" asked Sergeant Dante.

"He's taking the body to Rome, and the post-mortem will be done straight away. Won't know till then." Gadda looked at a pile of banknotes on the table before locking them away in a steel case. "Why all that money?"

Dante had no answer.

"All these women," muttered Gadda. "Who's Van Dam?"

"A friend of Mrs. Backhouse. Dutch Australian. A visitor to Italy. He's got a bad cold and has gone back to bed."

"You didn't see Mowbray himself?"

"He's suffering from shock. One of the women gave him a sleeping-tablet and I didn't disturb him."

"He can sleep on for a bit." The *commissario* rustled papers, then looked up. *"Bene.* And what happened, Dante? *You'd* know by now!" He said it patronisingly, but he knew Dante as a good fox-terrier. By mid-afternoon, Dante had produced useful notes on the whole party.

Dante gestured expressively. He was very excited.

"Signora Backhouse," he ventured. "And Backhouse is covering up for her. She's rich and spoilt and thinks she can do anything. Or else Mowbray. He was heard quarrelling with his wife just after dinner. Everyone knew of Backhouse's *relazione* with Raffaella Mowbray."

"A crime of honour! Mowbray's an Englishman, don't forget!"

Dante was from Calabria, fatalistic and handsome, with smouldering black eyes.

"Do you know what Barbicinti just told me?" Dante practically stammered in his eagerness to get the words out. "Someone loosened a wheel on her Simca, back in Vicovaro. She was nearly killed."

"Accident!"

"They met in Vicovaro. Mowbray wanted to show them a church. Then they went on to Subiaco, where they spent the night."

"Why Subiaco?"

"Convenience. Mowbray wanted them to see San Benedetto. Also, he wanted to make sure they all arrived up here at just the right time to see the frescoes with the light of the setting sun on them.

"Raffaella Mowbray had put her old Simca in for servicing the day before the tour started. Not far short of Vicovaro, Hedda Hardegen's Lancia overtook Signora Mowbray's Simca. Hardegen had Van Dam and Beverley Backhouse with her. They saw the back wheel on the Simca was very loose. When they got up to Vicovaro, Van Dam tightened the wheel and checked the others. But after that, someone must have loosened one of the *front* wheels."

"Hmm. Get Van Dam, will you?"

"He's got a terrible cold."

"Well, I'm not going to him," snapped Gadda. "And while you're fetching him, I'll see Beverley Backhouse."

When Beverley came in, Gadda said abruptly:

"Tell me about your trip to Vicovaro."

Beverley stared at him in surprise, forcing her mind back to that crazy drive two days before . . .

Starting out late, she and Hedda had overshot the turn-off for Vicovaro by some twenty kilometres and followed secondary roads which cavorted over the wild Abruzzi mountains. She had hung admiring and fearless at Hedda's side, and Hedda had driven like one possessed, in a sort of fury—Beverley knew—at having Van Dam in the back. But Beverley had been near ecstatic. What she loved best in the world was sitting next to Hedda while Hedda drove—and through that landscape!

Savage grey-white boulders stuck up like tombstones on the mountain-sides, which bore the marks of centuries-old terracing, and over everything were the emerald stains and feverish glow of spring . . .

"Let's skip Vicovaro and all that crowd, Hed!"

Hedda had muttered: "Cut San Donato? I'm on."

Van Dam had protested harshly.

"Oh come. You must deliver me. Of course you're both coming. We're expected too."

"Are we lost, Heddy?"

Van Dam had sworn, his restless eyes turned up to an outlandish village of the Middle Ages clinging precariously to the top of a ridge. Would they ever reach their destination? They had so quickly gone back in time. Van Dam had grabbed the map and taken complete charge.

"We meet around three. We'll just make it." And he had given concise directions for reaching Vicovaro.

"Fermare? E per quale ragione?" Beverley said now, sulkily. She spoke Italian like a native. "There was no point in stopping."

Gadda gaped at her. Now that she was close up, he could recognise her beauty. No point in stopping?

"We didn't have that far to go. The Simca couldn't go very fast anyway. Hedda flashed her lights to warn her."

Van Dam came in at this point, clad in a dressing-gown and looking hellish.

Gadda said, in English:

"If Mrs. Hardegen drives that Lancia down in the courtyard, she must be competent with cars."

"She needs to be, the speed she keeps up," said Van Dam emphatically. "Oh, she's a first-class driver." In sight of the *autostrada* at last, Hedda had put the Lancia through an entry curve with a mastery of controlled drift that few drivers are capable of. "She knows all about cars," said Van Dam now, with some satisfaction.

"Why didn't she stop when she saw the wheel loose on the Simca?"

"I told her to," said Van Dam quickly. "All she did was flash her lights and scoot past the Simca. I leaned out and shouted to Raffaella Mowbray and pointed to the wheel. We soon left the Simca behind, though. As soon as we got up to Vicovaro I tightened the wheel on the Simca. *And* checked the other three."

Beverley said distinctly: "So *you* say."

Van Dam started and turned on her angrily.

"What the devil do you mean by that?"

Gadda perked up expectantly.

"You're implying Mr. Van Dam did something else?"

"I mean only that what he says can't be checked now," replied Beverley. She looked frightened.

Van Dam controlled his temper.

"When I'd finished with her car, all four wheels were perfectly secure," he said forcefully.

"Why didn't the Signora Mowbray drive with her husband?" asked Gadda.

"His car was overflowing with equipment—projector, slides, screen and so on," Van Dam explained, calm again now.

"What were the others doing when you got to Vicovaro?"

"They were inside the church at the end of the main square."

"Everyone?"

"All except Juliette Deneuve. She arrived in Vicovaro ahead of the others and began work on a painting. I think Mrs. Boot was with her. She travelled up with Juliette."

Gadda turned to Beverley.

"Were you and Mrs. Hardegen with the others at all?"

"We went into the church as soon as we got there," replied Beverley.

Van Dam said immediately: "I didn't see you come out with the others."

Beverley gave him a long look, full of hostility. For a time she had been a helpless victim in his hands. Hatred, which had always played its part in their violent encounters, had now ousted sex. She knew him for a cruel man.

"Go and get Mrs. Hardegen," said Gadda to Dante.

When she appeared, Gadda said to Hedda:

"So, Mrs. Hardegen, you see the loose wheel, you and Van Dam and Mrs. Backhouse. One of you got the idea of a repeat performance. Who, I wonder?"

Hedda said nothing. If anything, thought Gadda, she was even better looking than Beverley Backhouse. A loving God had traced *her* outlines.

Gadda snapped at her:

"Why wouldn't you stop when you saw Raffaella Mowbray had a loose wheel? Your passengers wanted you to."

Van Dam snorted derisively.

"*I* wanted her to. I said so. *Mrs. Backhouse's* precise words were: 'Oh screw Raffaella. We're nearly there anyway.' "

"I will have Mrs. Hardegen's version, thank you, sir." Gadda turned cold eyes to Van Dam before addressing Hedda again.

"Did you and Mrs. Backhouse stay with the others in Vicovaro?"

Hedda quivered, reliving that brief interval inside San Giacomo, which had closed like an icy hand upon them. Musty with incense and shrouded in gloom, it had driven them out in search of coffee. They had walked, she and Beverley, up through the seedy handsomeness of the huge piazza, juke-box music blaring from half a dozen different bars. And Beverley had told her, then, that John Backhouse wanted a divorce. *"Make the most of this weekend, Heddy. It might be the last . . ."*

"Did you, Mrs. Hardegen?"

"No," said Hedda. "Only at first in the church. It was so cold, we . . . went and had a drink."

"And then?"

The beautiful eyes wandered from the *commissario*'s face.

"We went back to the Lancia and waited there," said Hedda.

"And the accident was just out of Subiaco?" Gadda asked Dante, later.

"Two or three kilometres from Subiaco. They had coffee and something to eat in Vicovaro, and then drove to the monastery of the Sacro Speco above Subiaco. It was closed, though. So they drove towards Jenne, to enjoy some scenery. They drove something like fifteen or twenty kilometres to a point high in the mountains where they stopped at a look-out. Then turned round and went down to Subiaco. Raffaella Mowbray was the last to leave. She was a long way behind the others. No one saw the accident."

Gadda drummed nervous fingers on his little table.

"I suppose I'd better see Backhouse," he said finally.

"Barbicinti is anxious to see you."

"The gallery manager?"

"*Già.* He is in a terrible state. He told me it was incredible anyone could have wanted to kill her. She was so beautiful and sweet. He was almost incoherent. Beautiful and sweet, and he said her laugh was joy and happiness itself. His very words!"

"Hmm." Gadda looked unimpressed. "I'll see Backhouse first."

Dante, about to dive round the screen, paused:

"There's one of the women who could be useful. Mrs. Boot. A real *ficcanaso,* but she has almost no Italian. Bursting with information, but she had to rely on one of the other women to interpret for her. Lady Loftus it was, and *she* was all concerned *not* to talk."

"All right. Get Mrs. Boot first. And then phone through to headquarters and warn them about the post-mortem. About the only good thing in all this," added Gadda dismally, "is that the telephone is still working. A chance in a hundred that the cable left the line of the road just above the landslide."

Alone behind the Chinese screen, Gadda waited, in his makeshift office, for Doris Boot.

XIII

"So, Signora Boot . . ."

The *commissario* raised his eyes to Doris and leaned back in his chair. His lips were very red in his pale face, Doris noted, and when parted in speech drew back from his long, even teeth in a slightly animal fashion. Only hair was lacking, thought Doris in surprise. If he grew a beard, it would come right up to those red lips and he would look like a—

"Did you know that Mrs. Backhouse habitually carried a gun?"

Doris jumped.

"We all knew. We'd all seen it."

"You mentioned a good deal of drinking had been going on. Was Mrs. Backhouse drunk?"

"She acted a bit tipsy, but I think myself she was consumed by jealousy." Doris paused impressively. "She didn't join us for cocktails before dinner. Of course, she and Hedda Hardegen act sort of superior. And they're always together."

"Mrs. Hardegen is a special friend of hers?"

Doris gave an unpleasant little smile.

"*Very* special, I'd say."

Dislike and synthetic encouragement fought for mastery of the *commissario*'s face. He looked down at his notes briefly before continuing.

"I regret having to ask such questions," he said. "Somehow I must get a clear picture of the people up here and what happened before Signora Mowbray's death. I have great need of an observant, unbiased witness such as . . ." he laughed gently, ". . . you are yourself."

Doris's eyes slid off at a tangent and she gave a complacent smile.

"What was the trouble over dinner you mentioned?"

"Well, everyone had been talking about art of course. Raffaella looked all tensed up and no wonder, with Barbicinti across the other side of the table."

"Barbicinti?"

"Well, it was obvious he couldn't keep his eyes off her."

"Go on."

"He was her *other* boyfriend. Up in Subiaco, night before last, I saw Barbicinti coming out of her bedroom."

The sun, bursting suddenly from behind a bank of cloud, flooded the "office" with a golden glow, bringing to sudden life the silken colour in Mowbray's screen and gilding the dark-browed little figure with the mean lips sitting opposite the *commissario*. To the latter there came suddenly the picture of Renato Barbicinti, racked by sobs, as Gadda had caught him earlier. His eyes fell on the photograph of Raffaella which lay before him. It had been supplied by her husband. Did Mowbray always carry a framed photograph of his wife with him? It showed a grave, gentle face, with level brows and eyes full of understanding. He put from his mind the set face of the corpse with the neat hole in the temple and tried to imagine Raffaella as she would have been in life. Would she not have had calm and limpid eyes, and smooth, slow, graceful movements with something of languor in them? That generous, full body, the large soft hands that promised tenderness. She would, he felt, have been a receptive woman. Would not that fair hair have glowed gently in the sunlight? And her laugh, when it came, was "joy and happiness itself." Three men had loved her—Mowbray, Backhouse and Barbicinti. Who would have wanted her dead?

Abruptly, the golden light was extinguished as the bank of cloud swamped the sun, leaving the partitioned room in semi-darkness. With an impatient movement, the *commissario* looked round for an electric light point which did not exist, and then barked at his clerk:

"Get another lamp from somewhere or some candles." He turned to Doris: "What did the Signora Mowbray actually say over dinner?"

"She managed to offend Juliette properly," Doris snapped, "going on about modern painting and how rubbishy it is. Raffaella had a very uppish sort of manner. Juliette got all worked up and began crying."

"A tempestuous sort of reaction."

"Well of course, she's French. She was extra touchy at Raffaella's remarks because only a few weeks ago she missed a big sale of one of her paintings in Barbicinti's gallery all because of Raffaella. Juliette told me so herself."

"Is that so?"

"A rich American was going to buy one, but he heard Raffaella giving some of her opinions about it."

"Really! And could you remember just what Mrs. Backhouse said last night over dinner?"

Doris embarked on a remarkably detailed account of Beverley's words, only a little embroidered, ending with a little snort:

"The old green-eyed monster at work there. Mind you, Beverley Backhouse has certainly been consoling herself. André Van Dam, for instance, only came up here because *she* brought him. She's very loose in her behaviour . . ."

"But you were implying, surely, a moment ago, that Mrs. Hardegen . . ."

"Even for these immoral times," said Doris solemnly, "I would call it scandalous. She arrives up here in the same car as her girlfriend, with her boyfriend as *well*. There's simply no *limit*. Oh," Doris caught herself up. "I nearly forgot. There's one thing could be very important. I caught Hedda Hardegen scrubbing what looked like grease off her hands in the washroom at Vicovaro. And she rounded on me like a tigress when I asked her what it was."

"You mean she could have been at the wheel on the Simca?"

Doris nodded. "Er . . . I hope you won't let on it was *me* that told you . . ."

"Certainly not. Now, Mrs. Boot—the evening in the Subiaco hotel. Tell me what happened. If you can, people's reactions to Signora Mowbray being overdue. In detail."

"Yes. My room in the hotel looked out over the main piazza. Juliette shared it with me." Doris was in her stride now, with a gratified look on her face. "I just happened to be leaning out, when Renato Barbicinti arrived in his smart new sports car. He hadn't been able to leave his gallery until afternoon, and he drove straight from Rome.

"I could see something was wrong by the way Professor Mowbray was striding up and down. And then suddenly Jo Ann Partridge burst into our room."

Doris stopped, her eyes narrowing as she recalled these events. She had witnessed a reaction not far short of electric from at least three people to Raffaella Mowbray's failure to appear.

"Have you seen Raffaella Mowbray? She's more than an hour overdue!"

Juliette, for one, had nearly knocked Doris over in her eagerness to get out of the bedroom. Downstairs, Renato Barbicinti had raced for his car. André Van Dam had followed him.

"I'd better come with you."

Renato had reacted violently to this suggestion. When Van Dam insisted, Barbicinti had actually pushed Van Dam away, slammed the door of his car on him and departed with a roar.

"Van Dam staggered back cursing. Juliette told him to take her car, but Van Dam let it go."

"It seems Van Dam had taken over the role of the Signora Mowbray's protector," suggested the *commissario.*

"We all noticed he was making a dead set at Raffaella," said Doris. "He was Beverley's friend, but we could only assume he and Beverley had quarrelled."

"What was Hedda Hardegen doing while all this was going on?"

For the first time, Doris looked uncomfortable.

"She was in her bedroom. With Beverley Backhouse."

"Are you sure?"

"Completely." Doris shrugged. "It was the room next to Juliette's and mine, separated by a bathroom. Both rooms opened on that bathroom."

"If Mrs. Hardegen had loosened that wheel," mused the *commissario* encouragingly, "she would surely have taken care to be down in the piazza to learn what happened . . ."

"She was in the bedroom, with Beverley."

Doris had turned red in the face.

"You heard them?"

"I *saw* them. And . . ." Doris wrenched out the words. "I couldn't possibly tell you what I saw!"

The two of them, in front of the room's huge, full-length mirror.

Doris had without a doubt blushed scarlet all over. The *commissario* had to wait a moment before she muttered:

"One thing I can tell you; Hedda was half mad at the prospect of Beverley Backhouse leaving Rome."

"I see . . . Yes, I see. And, since no one knew anything—I presume—about Barbicinti's attachment to Raffaella Mowbray . . ." mused the *commissario*.

"That's right." Doris's violent flush was receding a little.

"How did Mowbray treat his wife?" pressed the *commissario*. Doris gave him a sharp look and licked her lips.

"He's got beautiful manners—flippant, like, sometimes, but anyone could see he was fond of her. He didn't like her driving that old car up in the mountains. But he used to treat her very offhand, when she was showing the slides, especially when she got them mixed up. *But*—last night, things . . . blew up."

"Yes?" interpolated the *commissario* encouragingly.

And once more, Doris launched into a detailed account of the quarrel between Mowbray and his wife.

"I was taken aback, when Raffaella accused old Mowbray of having a girlfriend too. And a peasant! You could imagine him with an educated girl, but a peasant!"

"Hmm. Perhaps . . . well, never mind. She actually said she was leaving Mowbray for Barbicinti?"

"That she did. 'I'm marrying Renato,' she says. 'I want a man, not a fanatic who cares for nothing but his books, his pictures, his Bellini.' "

"What?"

"Bellini—he's a famous Italian painter." Doris was smug. "Mowbray has a painting by him in his study at home. I expect that was what his wife meant. I peeped in once, before a class. Juliette told me it was a Bellini."

"When did they have this quarrel?"

"Let's see. I listened to *Canzonissima* on Augusto's transistor in the ante-room shortly afterwards. The programme begins at eight-thirty. I suppose I heard the Mowbrays about ten minutes before that. I was probably in the ante-room listening to *Canzonissima* for two or three minutes. Then I went back to the sleeping quarters. The girls told me they'd heard *Canzonissima* too. There's a sort of echo that carries noises through from a place in the kitchen. Oh, before I went back I spoke to Mr. Backhouse by the fire."

"You joined him in here?"

"He came and sat in here for a few minutes after his dinner. I said a few words to him, I remember." Doris's voice was slightly sulky. "And after a minute he got up and walked out of the hall. Quite rude he was really, when I'd only been trying to be friendly. Seeing him sitting all by himself by the fire, with his head in his hands, I thought he might've appreciated having a little chat. But off he went as if a hundred devils were after him."

"Nothing more before the lecture began?"

"No. I rested until then. I went right off to sleep, as a matter of fact. It was the aspirin. I must have fallen into a deep sleep, because I don't think I'd have heard the bell if it hadn't been for Juliette tapping on the door to see if I was ready."

"You all went in together?"

Doris shook her head.

"I went in later. It was nearly half-past nine when the bell went, and by the time I got there this hall was all in darkness and the slide show was already on . . ."

"Signora Mowbray was helping with the slides when you entered?"

"No, she had left by the time I came in."

"And Dr. Mowbray worked the slide machine himself?"

"Yes." Doris sounded a little uncertain. "I think I must've dropped off to sleep again in the lecture, because when Mowbray finished with the slides I remember waking up with a jump and he said to me, "So you're resting, Madame?" and pretended to be angry. He's sort of very theatrical when he's in his stride. And everyone laughed. Cheap sort of way of getting a laugh, if you ask me."

"It would certainly seem so," agreed the *commissario*, soothingly and hypocritically.

XIV

"So, Mr. Backhouse, you are English, aged forty-nine, and you work for a banking organisation called the Anglo-European Banking Consortium?"

Commissario Gadda was a shock to Backhouse. He was young, not more than thirty. Pale, contained, broad of shoulder, sitting there at the table. But all the same he had the odour of a quiet authority. No one could possibly have guessed how wretchedly nervous Gadda was underneath, and largely on Backhouse's account.

"You're English?" countered Backhouse.

"I speak English, Mr. Backhouse."

"Not like an Italian. And you don't look Italian."

So Backhouse was a bully. Gadda stifled a sharp retort and said coldly: "My question is to be answered." His keen grey eyes glittered.

Gadda spoke English better than a lot of Englishmen, so his wife Rose said—fluently, even with elegance, his accent present only in an occasional un-English scurry or else a drawling of the vowels. Rose came from Nottingham, where she had been a schoolteacher. For ten years Gadda had studiously spoken English at home. Backhouse, after as many years in Italy, hadn't bothered to acquire Italian.

"Your information is correct," Backhouse was saying now. He cleared his throat impatiently. His eyes, behind black horn-rims, never left Gadda's face.

"Why did you take four hours to get up here from Subiaco?" asked the *commissario.* "Your BMW could have done it in far less than a third of the time."

"The engine was giving trouble for a while. I don't know what was wrong. Something to do with the electrics perhaps. Finally it went all right."

"And this explains your very late arrival?"

"I've just said so. When I got up here I sat in the car waiting for the rain to abate. Is this really relevant to your enquiry?"

The *commissario*'s pencil snapped in two.

"You were found in possession of the gun. Your position is very serious," he rapped out.

Only because he spoke English had Gadda been sent up here. But had his chief known already that Backhouse had been caught with the gun? If so, Gadda had not been told. His chief had said to him: "I imagine you'll be able to release Backhouse straight away. It would be very embarrassing to certain negotiations important to Italy which are about to take place with the Consortium if he were—er, involved in any substantial way in this event in the mountains."

The *commissario* threw the broken end of the pencil on the table and continued more moderately.

"The gun is yours?" He motioned towards a box on the table.

"Not exactly. If it is the gun which I think it is, it is my wife's actually. I bought it for her a couple of years ago. I travel a great deal and she is nervous at nights and when she comes home alone to an empty apartment. The maids do not sleep in. We're on the first floor, with enormous terraces."

The first floor. The *piano signorile* of course. Backhouse oozed prosperity. Dante's notes traced a success story indeed— a steady progression from one attainment to the next. The bold, aquiline nose, the aggressive manner were in keeping.

"Did you bring the gun up here with you?"

"No." John Backhouse compressed his lips, then opened them decisively. "When I got up this morning," he stated, "at about six-thirty, I saw what seemed to be my wife's gun lying on a window-ledge in the corridor outside the bedrooms."

"How did you recognise it?"

John Backhouse frowned and cleared his throat in a peculiarly unattractive fashion before replying.

"You mistake what I said. I said only that it seemed to be my wife's gun. The model is not particularly common."

"You inspected the number?"

"No, I didn't."

"You did not realise, Mr. Backhouse, that a bullet had been fired from your wife's gun?" The *commissario* spoke very deliberately.

"I did not."

"Ah no, of course, Mr. Backhouse, you could not know that."

The *commissario*'s apparently pointless rejoinder made Backhouse redden, and a vein stood out on his forehead, but he said, merely:

"I checked that the safety-catch was on, that was all."

"And you took the gun out to your car and locked it away without checking with your wife?"

"I did not wish to disturb her."

"And you tell me, Mr. Backhouse, that it was quite by chance that you had anything to do with this gun, which is your possession, or rather your wife's, and with which—it seems certain—a murder was committed during the course of the night?"

The clearing of Mr. Backhouse's throat then was very obtrusive, producing much coughing and the sort of snort which comes from trying to clear blocked antrums. During this the *commissario* waited, his eyes never leaving the other's face.

"No, it wasn't by chance. That feller Van Dam told me he'd seen a gun on the window-ledge."

"When was that?"

"Just after I got up here last night."

"And you checked on it?"

"It had already gone from the ledge."

"I see. Did your wife put the gun on the ledge?"

"She did not. The gun disappeared from her handbag last night shortly after she got up here."

"So when you saw the gun this morning—or what seemed to be your wife's gun—you immediately locked it in the boot of your car without a word to her or anyone else!"

"It was very early. No one else was up. I went for a walk."

"I see. When did you return?"

"Between nine-thirty and ten. More like ten. When I got in here, they were all standing round . . ." Backhouse's face grew very grim.

"Shortly after this you decided to get rid of the gun."

"You can put it like that. If I say I wanted to have a closer look at the gun and preserve any fingerprints on it before that pack of fools got their hands on it, I don't suppose you'll believe me."

"Is that a statement?"

"I hadn't decided what I was going to do. Obviously, if that gun were found in my car, I would be in a pretty sticky situation. But if the gun were still fully loaded, there was nothing to worry about."

"It was your intention to get rid of the gun if an inspection showed it had been recently fired, which for an experienced person would not be impossible to determine. Or perhaps your wife may have been carrying extra bullets, and the gun could become 'still fully loaded' once more."

The *commissario*'s tone was cutting. John Backhouse bit back an angry exclamation and merely said:

"For the moment I have no more to say."

The *commissario* rapped out an order in Italian to his clerk. For some moments a rapid stream of Italian filled the air as the clerk took down directly on the typewriter the *commissario*'s version of the interview. John Backhouse was left sitting there, with ill grace, shifting about in his chair and scowling at the pair of them.

At last they were done, and the *commissario* turned back to him.

"Why did Signora Mowbray resign from the Consortium?"

Backhouse frowned.

"She didn't. Her appointment was terminated while I was away."

"For what reason?"

"I had to have an Arabic-speaking person. There had been a reshuffle of staff and my new work has taken me increasingly to North Africa and the Gulf area. There was very little left for her to do."

"The *signora*'s work had been satisfactory?"

"Yes. But I don't speak Arabic myself, and the project I am now dealing with is very important, entailing continuous correspondence and report-writing in English and Arabic. Personnel decided it was easier to make the change in my absence."

"The *signora* took her dismissal hard?"

Backhouse shrugged.

"She was giving up a good deal of money. Our organisation pays its staff very well."

"I see. After five years." The *commissario* said the words quietly.

There was silence for a moment, the *commissario* intent on the arc of his fingers on the desk before him and Backhouse glowering at the other's impassive face.

"What exactly is your position in the Consortium?" asked Gadda.

"Sir William Loftus is managing director," replied the other stiffly. "I am his deputy and I have recently taken charge of the biggest investment project ever financed by the Consortium. You may have heard of it. We call it LETDEB for short."

"LETDEB! What does that mean?"

"Let the Desert Bloom. It's a project to render lands in North Africa fertile and productive—lands which for centuries have been invaded by the desert—by the use of advanced agricultural technology, large-scale desalinisation of sea water, afforestation. It is a vast, historic project and a long-term one. In the course of the preparatory work, oil and natural gas have been discovered." Backhouse paused and then continued quietly. "Italy hopes to contract part of those supplies."

"Yes, I see." The *commissario* refused to allow his knowledge of the importance of Backhouse's project for Italy to show in his treatment of him. "We will leave it at that for the moment. I will let you have a typed copy of your interview for signature. You read Italian? By law it must be in Italian, but if you desire, there may be an attested translation in English, at your expense."

John Backhouse rose to his feet and stood looking down at Gadda for a moment before he said deliberately:

"I should appreciate a lift to Rome in your helicopter. I've some very urgent business down there."

The thinly disguised command to a subordinate! The *commissario* clenched his teeth and said coolly:

"Give you a lift? I am afraid it is quite out of the question."

Backhouse breathed heavily.

"I wonder if you realise just how important it is for me to get back."

"I am afraid that the normal lives of all of you will be subject to interruption for a while."

Backhouse's face darkened.

"Don't you see—" he began angrily, then stopped and went on more calmly. "Hundreds of millions of dollars are already involved in this project, which is at a very critical stage of planning. My Consortium, as its name indicates, represents a number of important banks of North America and Western Europe, which together with the Arab oil states put together large parcels of money to finance projects to their mutual benefit and to provide the necessary technical and organisation inputs. Italy is to supply much of the technical help and capital equipment in return for long-term contracts for oil and natural gas. As you know, I got back from North Africa only yesterday morning, where I held a meeting of the top technical people who are advising on the overall plan of the project. They are due to meet again in Cairo next week, when we shall finalise our recommendations to the governments concerned. I have no time to waste with you, Commissario."

Gadda felt a positive hatred of Backhouse at that moment. For his own part, he was just back from England, where he had been sent to a police seminar on developments in technical aids to detection. He had been well treated and had returned with a store of good feeling for the British. Now Backhouse, with his cold arrogance, was destroying his vision.

"Nevertheless, Backhouse, it is quite impossible to allow you to return to Rome." Gadda relished silently his deliberate rudeness.

John Backhouse tensed himself and his chin jutted out.

"I want my briefcase, you damned fool. Then I could carry on working?"

"Where is it?"

"In my apartment."

"Surely someone in your office could get it and have it brought up here."

"These papers are top secret," said Backhouse patiently. "My briefcase is locked in my safe in the apartment."

"If you care to give me the key to your safe—"

"It's a combination lock."

"The combination, then . . ."

"Impossible. The fate of governments could be affected by the premature disclosure of material in my briefcase." He paused. "Governments whose goodwill is essential to this country of yours."

"I see. Well, Mr. Backhouse, failing what I suggest," said the *commissario* levelly, "I am afraid that you will have to consume your soul in patience while you ponder on the fate of governments."

With difficulty Backhouse swallowed words ready to burst out. He turned on his heel. Just as he was about to disappear behind the screen, the *commissario* called him back.

"I have another question for you, Signore. If your work was so pressing, why did you come up here at such a late hour yesterday? You must have realised you would need to stay overnight."

"Nobody can work all the time, Commissario. I wanted a break. I intended to return to Rome this afternoon and start work."

"You are an art-lover?"

"Eh? I suppose so, when I have time for it," the other grunted.

"You enjoyed the lecture last night?"

"I didn't go. Too tired," said Backhouse shortly.

"Of course." The *commissario* was busy doodling with another pencil. As Backhouse turned on his heel again, Gadda said:

"They are quite exquisite, the frescoes, are they not?"

"Eh? I suppose so. Haven't had a chance to look at them yet."

"Not this morning before the others were up?"

Backhouse snapped:

"No, I didn't go down to them."

He turned and this time disappeared round the screen.

Not given to sparing his inferiors, the anxiety of Gadda's chief, translated into nervous rage, crackled over the long-distance telephone wires.

"I've had nothing but phone calls about Backhouse."

"You know he was found with the murder weapon . . ."

His chief groaned and gave vent to a string of oaths.

"How is he taking it? Being questioned and all that?"

"Badly. He's moving heaven and earth to get to Rome, and I doubt if it is to get his papers, as he maintains. He has a well-filled attaché case with him." Gadda paused and said tentatively: "I think his apartment should be searched."

"Santo cielo!" The telephone clattered unpleasantly. "I've had at least three calls from Sir William Loftus, as well as one from the Ministry of Foreign Affairs and one from the British Embassy, all demanding that Backhouse be released immediately. It's impossible. The *giudice istruttore*—"

"I listened to him for half an hour this morning." The *commissario* glared at the wall in front of him.

"He is *most* reluctant to hold Backhouse—"

"Backhouse only got up here last night," pointed out Gadda. "He couldn't have got back to Rome much before this evening."

"The utmost pressure is being put on me," barked the telephone. "I can only warn you, Gadda, that although officially the *giudice* has entrusted the handling of this case to you, he is of the opinion that Backhouse should be released. How can I give you official support?"

"Forty-eight hours." The *commissario*'s hand clenched on the receiver. "Give me forty-eight hours. It can't make that much difference to the Consortium's affairs . . ."

"I am assured . . . a considerable difference." The telephone crackled alarmingly and the *commissario* held it away from his ear.

At the first opportunity Gadda said:

"His apartment is in Via Guerrieri. First floor. Number sixty-two, *interno* three. Two enormous terraces, four french windows opening on to them. No alarm, no bars. Maids go off duty at five p.m. Terraces are concealed from neighbours by trees in side garden. For Montanaro it would be child's play to get in."

"You'll take full responsibility for this yourself," said the voice at the end of the line coldly. "I know nothing about it." Then, reluctantly, "I'll get Montanaro to call you."

The *commissario* talked on for a few minutes, then replaced the receiver. He swallowed. A small point gained. A vital one, he suspected. A vital one towards solving the case. But if Backhouse—or his wife—were found guilty, it could be Gadda's own head that would roll.

XV

"Sit down, Madame Deneuve."

Even though coming into the "office" entailed only rounding the corner of a screen, Juliette still made a pathetic attempt at an entrance, holding out her hand as if being formally introduced, just as though the *commissario* had not come upon her three minutes before sitting alone in an obscure spot on the terrace outside, muttering away to herself as she stared fixedly into the distance.

"This is a terrible thing which has happened, Monsieur."

Almost as if she were giving him an opening for conversation on a purely social occasion! But her hand was trembling.

"When did you last see the deceased, Madame?"

"To speak to, then during dinner last night. I did not see her after she left the lecture."

"I am told that during dinner Signora Mowbray addressed some critical remarks to you about modern painting, which caused you great distress."

"Indeed!" Juliette drew herself up haughtily and flushed, while her hand sought a long string of pearls which nestled in the frills of her blouse. What a beautiful skin—like a ripe peach, wasn't it, with that flush upon it. "It was uncalled for, yes, what Signora Mowbray say. But if you think therefore that I make of her my mortal enemy, this . . . this is absurd!"

In no time she had become a little breathless and her chest—a full and admirable chest, he noted—heaved with emotion.

"Come, Madame. I wish merely to reconstruct a picture of the poor young lady's last hours. In fact, it is Mrs. Backhouse's reaction to the Signora Mowbray's remarks which interests me."

"Beverley? She spoke in my defence, that is all, and if she has perhaps exaggerated, it is because we *all* are drinking very much."

"She accused Signora Mowbray of stealing her husband. Was that an exaggeration?"

"I do not know." Juliette's eyes, clear and brown, shifted slightly. "I hear a little gossip from the Consortium ladies, nothing more. Women are always talking among themselves." Juliette's hands fluttered. "I am not of the Consortium. How can I know such things? The Signora Mowbray—what do I know of her?"

"Madame Deneuve, a young woman had been brutally done to death, after a probable attempt had already been made on her life. What can you tell me? What was your opinion of her?"

Juliette's eyes wandered.

"Ah, poor girl. I say nothing against her. Nothing except this —she said some hurtful things about my paintings. Perhaps she wished to speak on a level with her husband, who is an authority. It is all."

"Would you say Dr. Mowbray had been fond of her?"

"Dr. Mowbray," Juliette faltered. "He treated her sometimes *avec désinvolture*, without ceremony, but it is apparent that he was most fond of her."

"Madame Deneuve, when Mr. Backhouse arrived last night, you were no doubt watching him closely. Was Madame Mowbray present?"

"He does not see her," Juliette burst out. "He does not look at her. It is most apparent he wishes to avoid her." She shrugged. "It is to be expected, no? His wife is present."

"For the matter of that, it is quite a mystery," suggested the *commissario* smoothly, "just why he turned up here at all, would you not say?"

Juliette's face was suddenly an arena for conflicting emotions.

"You ask me for opinions," she burst out suddenly. "It is unjust, this."

"There now," he said soothingly. "I will ask you for a solid fact. Did you notice anyone leave the lecture last night?"

He watched her eyes, which met his in frantic appeal for a second, before they dropped and she muttered:

"Madame Mowbray, she leaves the hall, then enters immediately Mrs. Boot, who takes a seat. Not five minutes after, two people leave, one after another."

"Who?"

"Mrs. Backhouse first. And after her, Mrs. Hardegen."

"Very good. Now after the lecture, Madame, you stayed here for a long time talking to Professor Mowbray, together with Signor Barbicinti, Signor Van Dam, Lady Loftus and Mrs. Bennett, oh, and also Mrs. Parsons. Signor Tsuda was also present. At about two-thirty a.m. you all went to bed. During the night, Madame, I suppose you heard or saw nothing which might help our investigation?"

"No." Juliette suddenly crimsoned. Her hand flew to her mouth. "Commissario, this is in confidence. You will understand it is highly embarrassing to me. The fact is, I was not alone during the night."

"I see," said the *commissario* evenly. "Well, Madame, there is no reason why this need be revealed. May I ask, however, for my own purposes, with whom you spent the night?"

Juliette cast down her eyes and whispered a name.

"You were in his room?"

"Yes."

"All night?"

"All night."

"Until when?"

"Until . . . some time after eight I suppose, when I returned to my own room to dress."

The *commissario* consulted his papers. "Ah yes . . . You have known the gentleman a long time?"

"No, no! Commissario, we are all subject to a little madness at times, no? Last night . . ." The tears welled and spilled, "was such an occasion—the prelude to this tragedy. A rare occasion, when the present is forgotten in the greatness of the past. A brilliant conversationalist, Professor Mowbray, and he raised our talk to . . . to a level of enchantment." Juliette bowed her head and wept in earnest. "One was excited beyond measure," she muttered brokenly. "One continued to drink."

"Una follia, allora, da partè Sua, Signora?"

"Appunto." Juliette raised her sorrowful face. "But *now*, I have my professional reputation to think of!" She gazed at him imploringly.

He muttered something soothing. Juliette, quite distracted, rose to her feet. At a sign from him, she turned and fled round the corner of the screen, while he sat looking after her speculatively.

Never had Gadda been treated to emotionalism of this extraordinary order. He had to see the police doctor now, but he would certainly talk to Madame Deneuve again—soon. She would break down—yes, she would break down.

XVI

Gadda, fresh from a consultation with the police doctor, found Barbicinti waiting outside his makeshift office, formed by the thick curtain and the Chinese screen. Barbicinti flung himself into a chair. His grey-blue eyes were anguished and he kept brushing back the luxuriant dark curls from his thin face. The *commissario* allowed him to unburden himself.

"There was another attempt on her life," Renato burst out. "In Subiaco. Someone loosened the wheel of her Simca."

"I am aware of it. Go on."

"I only joined the party that evening, in Subiaco. The accident had already occurred, on the mountain. Raffaella drove the rest of the way with me. She was afraid. Terribly afraid."

"You suspect someone?"

Barbicinti frowned.

"Van Dam tightened a *back* wheel when she got to Vicovaro. The garage mechanic in Rome had left it loose when he serviced the car the day before. Van Dam checked all the wheels, so he says. He could have pretended to tighten the front wheel but really have loosened it. Oh, another thing! Backhouse's wife said something over dinner last night. She accused Raffaella of stealing her husband."

"You knew of the relation between Mr. Backhouse and Raffaella Mowbray?"

"I knew *nothing*." Barbicinti's eyes darkened. "I'd never even seen Backhouse before last night."

"You were a close friend of hers, however?"

"Let me explain. I have only recently returned to Rome as manager of the Galleria Gianicolo. The gallery opened in November of last year. Previous to that I spent some years in São Paulo, Brazil."

"How long had you known the *signora?*"

"Ah, since we were both little more than children, in the north."

"So. And then you lost touch with her?"

The young man's face was suddenly withdrawn.

"Raffaella married. I went to Milano."

"The two events had a connection, I imagine."

"Commissario, I do not hide the fact that we were very good friends. At one time, when we were both very young, I wished to marry her." He shrugged. "There was no money," he said simply.

"And?"

"I did not see her again until I returned to Rome."

"She was a beautiful woman," said the *commissario* gently, watching the other closely.

Renato's hands clenched.

"She was not only beautiful. She was a good person, the sweetest of persons, with a great capacity—" He spoke wildly.

"I have not suggested otherwise," said the *commissario* sharply. "You lost no time in renewing your acquaintance with her in Rome, then."

Renato started.

"I made no special move to see her, until one day—quite by chance—she came into my gallery." His face grew brooding. "She came in with Mrs. Backhouse and Mrs. Hardegen."

"Ah! The day Juliette Deneuve missed selling a painting because of Raffaella's criticism!"

"Well, yes. But the very same day her work attracted the attention of Van Dam, who represents a firm in Sydney. He is buying several of her paintings."

"Have you known Juliette Deneuve for long?"

"A matter of six months. She was introduced to me by the director of the Brera in Milan. She worked there years ago."

"In what capacity?"

"Restoring paintings."

Gadda made notes on his pad and then asked:

"Did you see Raffaella Mowbray after the lecture last night?"

"No. A few of us stayed on talking. Mowbray was still wound up, after a brilliant lecture."

"Mr. Tsuda was present at this talk, *non è vero?*"

"Yes."

"Mr. Tsuda is very interesting to me." Gadda looked up. Barbicinti's eyes were suddenly entangled helplessly with the *commissario*'s. Gadda just did not smile. "He is the only one of you all who managed to get away from here, you see. Tell me, Signor Barbicinti, what you know of Mr. Tsuda."

With an effort Barbicinti wrenched his eyes away and said cautiously:

"Nothing of consequence. A pleasant man, well informed, indeed learned. Very interested in art."

"And he left this morning very early in his car, bound for—"

"I think, for Rome. He was in a hurry. I think he was to catch a plane to Paris, someone said."

"He was not attending the Rome lectures?"

"No. He was quite unknown to any of us. I believe he learned of the frescoes through his Embassy." Barbicinti had relaxed somewhat.

"A pity he is gone. There is nothing else you can tell me about him?"

Barbicinti shook his head.

The *commissario* took a paper from his table and ran his eyes over the contents. Then he looked direct at Barbicinti and rapped out:

"Why, then, did Tsuda write a letter to his bank in Austria— the Bankhaus Aschenbach, Wien, instructing them to open a numbered account in his name on which only you in person could draw?"

And Gadda tossed the paper across. Barbicinti had frozen, his eyes glued to the letter.

"I cannot think, Signor Barbicinti, that you were unacquainted with the gentleman."

Renato raised his eyes to the commissario's with a show of frankness.

"Signor Commissario," he burst out finally. "If I have concealed a connection with Mr. Tsuda, it is, I assure you, of no importance to your enquiry."

"Ah." The *commissario* waited.

"The fact is . . . the account is being opened for a very simple reason. It is a convenient way for Tsuda to reimburse me for certain works of art which I am to buy for him in Italian auctions. Tsuda is a wealthy man and an art collector . . ."

"Why did you not mention it?"

Renato's face quivered.

"As you know, we Italians have undeclared bank accounts abroad. Ready money in a strong foreign currency happens to be of great use to me."

"And you no doubt evade tax as well."

Barbicinti gestured.

"A minor, er, point . . ."

The *commissario* said softly:

"What I do not understand, Signor Barbicinti, is why a copy of this letter from Tsuda should have been found in the Signora *Mowbray*'s handbag."

Renato started.

"I cannot explain." His lips tightened, and his eyes darted away from Gadda's and then back. "But we were talking together, and I had mislaid the copy which Tsuda gave me. I can only think that Raffaella found it somewhere and put it in her bag for safekeeping."

"Ah." Gadda looked at him impassively. "One other question. Have you any idea why Signora Mowbray should have been carrying a large amount of lire with her?"

"No."

"Notes were found under her mattress."

Barbicinti shrugged.

"To pay for the accommodation here? There are twelve of us . . ."

"And thirteen with Tsuda, yes. Or there were . . ." agreed the *commissario*. "But even in our country a group of thirteen people would hardly be charged fifty million lire for lodging."

There came a thunder of footsteps and two policemen summarily burst round the screen.

"Commissario! Please come quickly!"

"What is it?" Springing to his feet, Gadda drew the men out of earshot.

And before he hurried off with them, Gadda strode back and barked at Barbicinti:

"Stay in this hall with the others. No one is to move out of it."

"What . . . what . . . ?"

"After all, you may not have the freedom of a foreign bank account, Signor Barbicinti," Gadda said roughly, "since your client has just been found in his own car . . . dead."

Second Act

XVII

About a kilometre down the road which spiralled down from the monastery in a succession of sickening hairpins, they found the Mercedes. It had swerved violently and left the road to tear through thick undergrowth down the bank. By a miracle it had not gone crashing headlong down to the River Aniene—five hundred metres below—but had been saved by a rocky outcropping overgrown with stout ilexes. The car had tipped on two wheels, smashed against one of the trees and settled, precariously, at an angle of ninety degrees. The front of the car was badly crumpled.

After a policeman had checked the car was stable, Gadda and the doctor clambered down. Mr. Tsuda was still strapped to his seat by a seat-belt but had slipped sideways and his head had struck the shatter-proof glass of the window. His left temple was covered with blood. His jaw was broken and his throat purple and swollen. He looked very small and frail against the massive strength of the Mercedes.

The police doctor spent a long time examining the body without moving it. Then he said to Gadda:

"Dead about six or seven hours, from the feel of him. That's taking into account lack of ventilation in the car, which would delay loss of body temperature." He fell silent for a long moment before adding:

"*Non va!* The impact was not great. He didn't break his jaw from it. He could conceivably have broken his neck when the car hit the tree—if he had been totally relaxed; that is, asleep—but he could not have been asleep. The car is built like a tank. And yet, his jaw is smashed in."

The doctor pointed to the dried blood on the abrasion on the left temple.

"This was made on impact, though—a comparatively slight wound." Gingerly, he put a finger on the abrasion. "Look at that. The blood all dried and brown and hard, like parchment." His sharp small eyes turned on Gadda. "He was already dead! He was already dead before his head struck the glass here. He was dead before the car crashed."

They left Tsuda to the photographer and climbed up again.

"Of course," Gadda gazed down the precipice, "the Mercedes should have finished way, way down there. A chance in a thousand the car got diverted on its way down the bank and finished against those trees. A freak finish. But for that, it might have ended in flames. Reconstruction would have been very difficult."

On the road, they searched patiently for tyre-marks. Newly paved, the surface yielded nothing. Only from the course of the car through the undergrowth did they fancy that it had been headed away from San Donato when it left the road. They could not be sure.

Gadda walked down to the landslide. It was an impressive sight. A giant hand had hurled down earth, trees and massive boulders, which covered what was left of the road. Great chunks of the road had given way. But they found distinct tyre-marks where the Mercedes had stopped, reversed and made off again up the hill.

Dante and a man from the *scientifica* met them as they walked back to the monastery. Dante was excited.

"I've found his spectacles. One lens smashed as though it had been trodden on, near where his car was parked. The spectacles are the duplicate of a pair in his suitcase. His vision was very poor. They are for a strongly myopic person. He couldn't have seen to drive a car without them."

A frail man of middle age. It would have been comparatively easy to overpower him. The blow which smashed his jaw could have been delivered by a man—or by a woman armed with what? The butt of a gun, a spanner, a bottle . . .

Tsuda had left at five a.m. all right and got as far as the

landslide. He had had to turn back. In the parking-lot down from the monastery, someone had killed him and tried to conceal his death by faking an accident to the Mercedes . . .

"Please get in touch with the Japanese ambassador and check on Tsuda," Gadda said later into the telephone. "Tsuda told someone the ambassador was a friend of his. Anything at all the Embassy knows of Tsuda. We know he has an apartment in Paris, in the Place Vauban, VIIe *arrondissement,* in front of the Ecole Militaire. Probably the Embassy could give you the telephone number. It begins 705 but I can't read the rest. He had on him an airline ticket for the Alitalia flight leaving Rome at two p.m. today. He hired the Mercedes on arrival in Rome two days ago. The Hertz documents are in the car.

"Ring his apartment in Paris and find out if there is anyone there called 'Al.' There are references to 'Al' in his diary. Find out why Tsuda came to Italy, and for only a few days.

"Then get in touch with the Bankhaus Aschenbach, Vienna, and find out on what terms Barbicinti was to draw on the numbered account opened by Tsuda with them. It's urgent. Interpol will be able to prevail. Barbicinti says he met Tsuda a few months ago in Rome and it was arranged then that he should act for Tsuda at auctions. He says they were introduced by a mutual friend in Rome. It may be so, but he never volunteered the information before a copy of the letter to the bank was found on Signora Mowbray. And Barbicinti was an old boyfriend of hers —perhaps her first lover. A relation recently renewed in Rome.

"You'll let me know the results of the two post-mortems at the earliest—"

At this point there was an interruption on the line and the head of the Sezione Omicidi broke in asking for the latest report.

"No one knew or heard a thing," Gadda said. "All slept soundly. There seems no link between the two deaths unless Mr. Tsuda was a witness of the woman's. But she was killed long before Tsuda left this morning, and Tsuda was with the others all last night and never left the hall till two-thirty a.m." Gadda sighed dolefully. "The only one who was up early was Backhouse. He says he woke about six-thirty, noticed the gun, and went down to his car to hide it. Then he went for a walk, reappearing only just before Raffaella Mowbray's body was discovered. We don't know when the gun was replaced on the ledge in the corridor."

Gadda stopped talking as frenzied noises came from the telephone receiver. He listened in silence for the most part. When the call was over he sat by the telephone for several minutes. If John Backhouse were guilty—or his wife, or both of them—anything could happen. Power told. Influence could divert justice. A scapegoat might be needed . . . He felt suddenly as though the life were being squeezed out of him, pressured as he was by his embarrassed superiors on one hand, by his own need to maintain professional integrity on the other.

"I am, of course, wondering if the two deaths are connected," said Gadda, as he put Mowbray into a chair behind the screen. Mowbray was so pale he reminded the *commissario* of a very tall and elegant ghost.

"Poor Tsuda appeared here quite independently," Mowbray said. "He was unknown to anyone here."

"He was known to Signor Barbicinti," Gadda remarked drily.

"No!"

"Barbicinti had arranged to act for him at Italian auctions."

"I knew nothing of it. Barbicinti certainly never mentioned it."

The *commissario*'s eyes were fast on Mowbray's face as he said:

"Your wife had fifty million lire in banknotes under her mattress."

"Impossible!"

"You know nothing of it?"

"Good heavens, no. It's an utter mystery to me!" Mowbray looked flabbergasted.

"Barbicinti," probed Gadda, "was a close friend of your wife's. In fact, he and she . . ."

"Yes." Mowbray waited with fear in his eyes for Gadda to continue.

When the *commissario* was silent, Mowbray added wildly:

"As you suggest, there was a strong attachment."

His long-fingered, beautifully shaped hands clenched on the arms of his chair.

He looked so wretched that Gadda did not insist.

"What do you know of Van Dam?" he asked, lamely.

Mowbray shrugged.

"He is buying some of Juliette's paintings. He represents some Australian art firm. Mrs. Backhouse asked if she could bring him up here."

"What about the ladies, the members of your class . . . ?"

"I am afraid I know very little about any of them. Hapless women! They have paid dearly for their mystification, however." Mowbray laughed mirthlessly. "Suffering cold, discomfort and now—tragedy."

"One member of your class, though, Mrs. Backhouse . . ."

Mowbray was silent, his head down.

"Dr. Mowbray, how long had you known about your wife and Mr. Backhouse?"

"Only for a few weeks past," answered Mowbray quietly. "Someone sent me an anonymous letter. It arrived at my apartment just after a lecture." With an expression of distaste, he took out his wallet and withdrew from it a folded paper, which he handed over.

"It was typed on good quality notepaper," commented Gadda, glancing at the brief letter. "You have the envelope?"

"No. I threw it away. It was unstamped." Mowbray's voice expressed all the scorn in the world. The veins stood out on his forehead.

"One wonders, of course, at that sort of mentality," murmured the *commissario*, watching the other closely.

"Soon after I got the letter," Mowbray was breathing heavily and a slight flush crept over his cheeks, "soon after, my wife told me that she wished . . . to leave me."

"For Backhouse?"

"For Backhouse, yes." Mowbray was gaining control of his face.

"And you . . . ?" the *commissario* pressed, gently.

"I asked her to wait, to think it over." Mowbray spread out his hands. "Commissario, she was young; Backhouse was a man very much older. A divorce is a terrible business. I felt also that

Backhouse himself, a married man, was at an age—well, at a very dangerous age."

"Let us return to this letter," suggested the *commissario*. "All the members of the class were present?"

"Yes. It was the first lecture I gave them." Mowbray's lips curled ironically. "A nice finale."

"And you had no suspicions?"

Mowbray was silent for a moment, staring into space. Then he shook his head.

"No," he said finally. "It seemed incredible that any one of them should stoop to such a thing."

"You knew Mrs. Backhouse carried a gun with her?"

Mowbray slowly focused. His eyes as they met the *commissario*'s were terrible. He nodded.

"You knew Mr. Backhouse before he came up here?"

"Of course. Raffaella and I had dined with him and his wife on a couple of occasions."

"Recently?"

"Oh no. The last occasion must have been several years ago. It was not a friendship in real terms. I was asked to their home purely as Raffaella's husband of course. Backhouse and I are also in very different fields."

"Mr. Backhouse is not interested in art?"

"Good heavens, no," Mowbray shuddered. "He is a practical man of affairs. An extremely competent specialist, I am sure, but a man who hangs the trash he does on his study walls . . . I hardly know why I remember it, except that I was once amused when he, knowing I was a devotee, took me in there specially to have a look at some of the worst tourist rubbish I'd ever seen, all very carefully and expensively framed."

"Yes?" The *commissario*'s mind wandered the least fraction, thinking of his own habit of picking up a cheap sketch or two of places he visited himself on business or on holiday, usually from a local street artist. He supposed that was tourist stuff . . .

"Yes," he said again. "I see. Tell me, Dr. Mowbray, what time did your wife leave the lecture last night?"

"I suppose about ten o'clock, perhaps a few minutes before. No, definitely before, I think. I remember we had just put on the Santa Trinità 'Nativity of the Virgin' . . ."

"Could you repeat that?"

"The 'Nativity of the Virgin,' a work of Lorenzo Monaco."

"Lorenzo?"

"The Camaldolese painter, Lorenzo Monaco," repeated Mowbray. "He painted many of the frescoes up here, of course." His faintly impatient tone mocked the *commissario*'s ignorance. "I would think she went out before ten o'clock because the 'Natività' was the sixth slide only for the evening."

"I see. You saw her again before you went to bed?"

"No. It was very late when we finished. That is, the lecture was over by about eleven-fifteen, but somehow or other we got talking. And we stayed up till all hours of the morning, a few of us. Barbicinti and I didn't go off to our beds until after two this morning. Naturally I did not disturb Raffaella, who was in the first cell as one enters the corridor, as you know."

"When did you first discover she had been killed?"

Mowbray's face trembled.

"Only after breakfast . . ."

"You did not look in on her this morning?"

"Yes I did. But her bed was made up. I imagined she had risen already . . . Commissario, when was my wife killed?"

"It is not yet known. At a guess, some time before midnight."

"When I went to bed," Mowbray's voice broke. "She was already . . ."

"I think so," said the *commissario* gently, noting the dark rings under Mowbray's eyes. Those eyes, which gazed at him with anguish.

"We must search your wife's possessions, you understand."

"You will go through the apartment?"

"It is necessary."

"I should be grateful if you would not touch or move the one or two things I have of value in my study. There's a little *kouros* of the sixth century standing on my desk, for example."

"A what?"

"A Greek archaic statue." Was there a hint of impatience this time in Mowbray's voice, underlying the torment? "And on the side-table a very small collection of Greek vases."

"They will be taken care of," Gadda promised. "That is all for now, Dr. Mowbray. I hope you may be able to get a little rest."

Rising to his feet, the *commissario* conducted Mowbray round the screen.

XVIII

At seven o'clock the police helicopter was once more on its way, this time with the addition of two covered stretchers. The police doctor and the photographer left with it.

"I suppose it's *safe* for you to leave," growled Gadda.

He put in a report for the *giudice istruttore* and stood for a few minutes out of range of the glistening whirr of the propellers, which had all the foliage waving wildly around him. He and Dante were now alone for the night on the mountain-side with a pack of frightened men and women—one of whom, or perhaps more than one of whom, had done murder. It had come on to rain again and was bitterly cold.

He turned and walked to the lower terrace. On the path above there was movement and he saw Mowbray approaching, a tall black figure in the swirling darkness, his coat flapping wildly in the wind like a cloak. Mowbray gazed over the more intense blackness of the valley as he walked. There was about him an enormous isolation. And as he came near, impassioned words fell from him, borne quickly away on the wind. The *commissario* stepped quickly aside into the cover of some bushes. But Mowbray didn't even glance at him as he passed.

Inside the big hall, Gadda could smell meat cooking. Dante told him Lucia had dinner ready. Would he like to eat first? It was warm in the kitchen.

The policemen were served by a frightened Lucia and her husband by the kitchen fire. Gadda hurried through and went out to the big hall.

"Living in a nightmare." Gadda just caught the words, uttered by one of the women, as he passed, and to look at their faces he could believe it. Most of them were by the fire. He hurriedly gained his little table behind the screen at the far end of the hall. There ensconced, he was virtually alone, undisturbed by the loudest of voices.

He had just time to see someone before dinner. Lady Loftus. She came round the screen full of English aloofness. So utterly entrenched behind that wall of reserve, so reluctant to allow that any member of the Consortium could be involved in these "unfortunate occurrences," so horrified at being questioned, that he might as well not have seen her. She had noticed nothing, seen nothing . . . She had, however, been on the telephone to her husband, who was, as the *commissario* knew, the managing director of the Consortium, and he had added his urgent plea that Mr. Backhouse be released immediately . . .

Doris, coming in through the main door, scuttled like a frightened rabbit past the screen and towards the fire. She went up to Juliette and handed her some keys.

"I didn't need them after all," she said. "One of the doors of the Peugeot was open anyway." She held out a bar of chocolate. "This was there, anyway. I think I know where André was this afternoon; in your car, I should think. There's no mistaking those Caporal cigarettes he's so fond of."

"So?" Juliette accepted a piece of chocolate. "I hope he has not left us his cold as well."

She looked drawn, and her eyes were anxious.

"Wonder we haven't all got colds by now," said Doris. "Still no food, and the temperature dropping." She shivered and bit into a piece of chocolate. "Just look at Renato Barbicinti. He's hardly sat down once. Nerves, I expect."

"Nerves," breathed Juliette. "Yes, of course, nerves." Her hand was on her heart, and Doris looked at her curiously.

"There he goes again." Doris watched Barbicinti, who had been restlessly pacing, disappear through the door leading to the sleeping quarters.

From behind the screen, Gadda saw Lucia appear with a pile of plates and a big tureen. He went quickly towards the cells. Backhouse. He wanted to see for himself what Backhouse was doing. Backhouse had stayed in his cell all afternoon, coming out only at rare intervals. He had one briefcase with him. He could have locked away papers indispensable to his work in his safe in the Via Guerrieri apartment, but Gadda was sure Backhouse had quite enough to go on with somehow. He had only once been in Backhouse's cell—a routine visit which had included all of them; and Backhouse, in a veil of smoke, had been bent over a little table, totally immersed in his work, or seeming so. He had twice gone for a brisk walk, two or three times appeared in his wife's company with a forbidding expression on his face. Was he really working in that little cell?

Further down the corridor Gadda paused at the sound of men's voices coming from a door slightly ajar.

"Just what the hell do you mean by poking round in my room!" came furious accents.

"I was *not* poking about!" came another voice.

"By God, I saw you! You were just closing my suitcase—"

"Take your hands off me!"

Gadda pushed the door open a fraction more. Van Dam stood menacingly over Barbicinti, who looked small beside him. Barbicinti, facing the door, noticed its movement, and Van Dam's hand dropped. As he swung round, the line of his jaw hard, Gadda saw a set of muscles move in his shoulder, under the thin dressing-gown he wore.

"If you please, Signori," said the *commissario* invitingly.

"He was searching my room," Van Dam snapped.

"This is true?" The *commissario* was looking at Van Dam with fresh eyes. He had spoken only briefly to him, about the wheel on the Simca. Van Dam's manner, his tone, he had found persuasive, with a ring of truth about it. Perhaps it had been the Dutchman's righteous disgust at the garage which had left the wheel on the Simca loose.

"I was only—inspecting Juliette's painting." Renato Barbicinti waved at the canvas which stood against the wall. "The door was open and I took the liberty . . ."

Van Dam suddenly retreated from his aggressive position.

"I suppose I'm suffering from nerves," he conceded, shrugging. "Forget it." He rubbed his face with the towel round his neck. "I've got a dose of flu that doesn't help."

A ghostly bell rang, a sound which seemed on another wavelength.

"Dinner," said Barbicinti.

"Where is that bell ringing?" asked Gadda.

"Off the kitchen. It's a trick of acoustics. Like wireless. From the rock. You hear it in all the cells."

"Yes, I remember." Gadda recalled someone telling him about the women listening to *Canzonissima.*

He waited until Barbicinti had gone off and Van Dam, hastily changing into jacket and slacks, had also left his cell. Backhouse had disappeared as well. None of the cells locked. Inside, a makeshift sliver of wood fitted into a slot when the occupant was in the room. Locks were scheduled, but had not yet been fitted. In turn, Gadda went quickly and efficiently through the contents of each, beginning with André Van Dam's. It did not seem that Van Dam had cause for anger at Barbicinti's intrusion. Any money, or papers, he had with him Van Dam must carry on his person. The only thing of interest in the cell was Juliette's canvas standing against the wall. In the half-light of the hurricane lamp, the russet and green and gold of the Italian countryside shone brightly, with an instant popular appeal the *commissario* had no trouble in appreciating. He stood for some moments admiring it.

Backhouse's cell contained a half-bottle of Ballantine's and a glass, a thick notepad, a bulky typewritten report entitled *Capital Requirements—Stage I: North African Regional Agricultural/Mineral Development Project.* Gadda had seen Backhouse carry a briefcase with him to dinner. Did he take it to the bathroom too?

Doris's cell, Lady Loftus's, Mrs. Partridge's, nothing of note. Beverley Backhouse's, Hedda's. Nothing again, except an array of gorgeous underclothing, a pair of shoes by Ferragamo—the sort of discreet elegance that costs the world. Juliette's: a litter of cosmetics and bottles on the bedside table, a suitcase untidily stuffed with clothing. But meticulously clean paintbrushes and a heavy wooden case containing orderly rows of tubes and bottles and brushes. A container for canvases. The two sides of Juliette.

Mowbray's cell had the coldness of despair—tumbled bedclothes where the poor man might or might not have snatched a little sleep, possessions thrown carelessly down. Lecture notes jotted down on a notepad in the sort of script that betrays a boyhood training in Greek.

Outside in the corridor Gadda inspected the high Gothic windows. Here, on the ledge, had lain the gun—secreted by whom? Used and replaced by whom? Retrieved finally by Backhouse.

Gadda stood stock-still for some minutes, deep in thought. Then, head down, a bear-like figure now in the half-darkness, he walked down the long corridor.

The shattering violence of the helicopter close overhead, an ugly sound suggestive of trouble, pulled them from sleep next morning.

Over breakfast, nerves were tense, conversation practically non-existent. Renato's finely drawn face, suited to high tragedy, was handsomer than ever. Van Dam was pasty and bad-tempered. Mowbray breakfasted in his room.

Jo Ann brought robust common sense to bear and announced that, if the *commissario* had no objection, she would take a long, bracing walk and would welcome company, though the company was very obviously only that of her intimate pal Louise Parsons.

Juliette, hands clattering the coffee cup against the saucer, said tremulously that she could not walk in these shoes, no, and that it was impossible to do nothing. She would go to her room and paint the view from her window. She would endure no longer without some work. And rapidly and resolutely she left the hall to put her plan into operation.

Beverley, who had found fleeting escape in the dazzlingly simple solution to all things, even death, of a dream-fantasy that was the converse measure of her despair, woke to daylight and nightmare reality.

Immediately after breakfast the *commissario,* with his cold eyes boring into her, with his astounding command of the English tongue, ordered her into his sanctum. Beverley gave Hedda a long look and without a word walked before him down the hall, a slim figure in black jumper and tight pants, the utter simplicity of which spelt *haute couture.*

Sitting down in the one chair, she turned her green eyes on

him. With no warning, the *commissario* handed her a glossy black-and-white enlargement, twenty by thirty centimetres, of a woman's head and shoulders. It had been mounted on a piece of fibre-board. The photograph was clearly recognisable as Raffaella but the face had been peppered with bullet holes.

All the colour left Beverley's face suddenly and her hand flew to her mouth.

"In your bedside table." Gadda's tone was deadly.

"You searched the apartment—"

"Naturally," he rapped out.

"You had no right!" she protested, white to the lips.

"Oh, yes. In Rome they found that the gun which killed the Signora Mowbray—your gun—was quite clear of any prints except those of your husband." The *commissario* paused. "They used to make effigies and stick pins in them," he suggested. "Same principle, no? Witchcraft. The sort of thing restricted to primitive people usually."

"I was only practising. You have to have some sort of Aunt Sally."

"You were practising." The *commissario* stared at her with something like horror.

Senselessly, she said, "Only in the country." Her voice choked on the words. "I used to go in the country." Her eyes slid somewhat wildly to one corner after another of the screen, as though she would suddenly run for it. She swallowed and licked her lips.

Gadda gave a smile, his red lips drawing back unpleasantly from his teeth, his eyes impersonal and cold.

"You lied to the sergeant about the time you left the lecture. You told him you were there until the end of it. In fact, you were seen to leave this hall shortly after Signora Mowbray went to bed, somewhere about ten o'clock. Why did you leave the lecture?"

"I . . . wasn't well. I'd had a lot to drink . . ."

"And yet this lecture was the high point of the whole visit."

She muttered an assent.

"I put it to you that you brought that gun up here. When the Signora Mowbray left the lecture you followed her, inveigled her out on the terrace on some pretext, shot her, pushed her over. You then wiped the gun clean and put it on the ledge in the corridor. Did you then spin some tale to your husband about the gun and ask him to hide it in his car? Or did you simply trick him into handling it and place it in the boot yourself in order to incriminate him?"

Beverley sat slightly hunched and still as if hoping his words would pass over her, leaving her unscathed.

"No." He could hardly hear her.

"Why did Signora Hardegen leave the lecture shortly after you?"

"She was tired."

Gadda suddenly lost patience. Springing up, he strode to the edge of the screen and bellowed in Italian to the policeman outside: "Get Signora Hardegen along here quick!"

When Hedda appeared he barked at her:

"You lied about the time you left the lecture Saturday night. Why?"

Before speaking she first exchanged with Beverley a long, grave look. Without words, something secret passed from one to the other.

"I wanted to make sure Beverley was all right."

"Whether she was all right," repeated the *commissario* contemptuously.

He picked up the photograph, glanced at it and threw it down on the table. Hedda's eyes widened and she caught her breath.

"In Mrs. Backhouse's drawer, beside her bed," sneered the *commissario*.

"Oh, but . . . that was simply a . . . a sort of joke, a joke of mine," Hedda said abruptly.

"I see. A joke of yours," he repeated scathingly.

"I was teaching her to shoot. We had to have a target. I said to her to use her special *bête noire*."

"You persuaded her to use this as a target?"

"Oh no," Beverley suddenly intervened. Her head went up. On Hedda's entrance, strength seemed to have poured back into her. "She didn't say that. I said it. She *never* wanted me to use the photograph. I thought of it. It was a crazy thing to do. Just one of those crazy things . . ."

"No, it wasn't like that," said Hedda obstinately, with a little shake of her head at Beverley. "I did suggest it to her."

The *commissario* tightened his lips and then said:

"Mrs. Hardegen, did you loosen the wheel on the Simca?"

For a split second Hedda's confidence left her.

"Mrs. Boot," said Gadda succinctly, "saw you washing grease off your hands in the washroom at Vicovaro—the only place where the car could have been tampered with."

"She didn't," Beverley cried immediately.

"You did yourself!" The *commissario* turned on her.

"No, I loosened her wheel." Hedda was white-faced, but she raised her chin and said coolly now: "Beverley had nothing whatsoever to do with any of this—she neither interfered with the Simca nor had anything to do with the killing of Raffaella Mowbray. Yes, she had a gun and she has been practising with it. And I was teaching her. She brought the gun up here but she never used it or even saw it—that is, after I took if from her handbag soon after we got up here."

"Ah! *You* took it from her bag." Gadda jumped to his feet, looking so threatening that Hedda shrank back.

"I put it on the ledge, high up where no one could see it. As I thought." Hedda was staring at him in terror and Beverley made as if she would clasp her in her arms.

"There are some people taller than you," said Gadda sternly. "Mr. Backhouse, for one."

"I never saw it again," insisted Hedda bravely.

There was a commotion outside and Backhouse, brushing aside a police officer, stormed round the screen.

"That's all right, come in Mr. Backhouse," said Gadda evenly. He was standing shielding the photograph but suddenly he moved so that it was visible. Backhouse's mouth opened and shut again. He stood there making the unwelcome deduction. The silence was long and oppressive.

"You found this when you got back from Africa, didn't you?" enquired the *commissario*. "The photograph was on the floor, the drawer was open and Saturday's edition of the *Daily American*, which you must have brought in yourself, was lying on the bed. You panicked, Mr. Backhouse, and came racing up here."

"You assume a lot, Commissario." His expression cleared and

Backhouse actually laughed. "Look here, the thing's ridiculous. I heard m'wife explaining about her using the photograph as a target. It was childish and distasteful on her part, admittedly, but certainly not criminal in intent. That so, Beverley?"

She assented, practically echoing his words as she looked at him just as she had looked at Hedda—with that look of utter submission that made the *commissario* grit his teeth.

"The gun has been checked by test-firing," stated Gadda. "There's no doubt it was the weapon used. There were no prints but your own, sir."

Backhouse shrugged.

"As I said before, the murderer must have wiped it clean of prints before putting it back on the ledge. Commissario," he added, possibly very aware of his commanding bearing and the advantage of his extra inches, "m'wife does not lie, nor do I, nor does Mrs. Hardegen. I heard what they both said."

The *commissario*'s face was rapt. Backhouse had decided that the girls' innocence was a necessity to him, that was all. To him, to his career, to the Consortium's affairs no doubt. Gadda, however, didn't have time to take it further, because just then Dante announced that Rome was calling urgently.

It was the police doctor, with the results of the post-mortem examinations. Raffaella's death could have occurred at any time between eight-thirty and midnight, though the doctor was inclined to put it earlier rather than later, probably between eight-thirty and ten o'clock. Tsuda had died as a result of the throat wound, in the early hours of the morning. The temple wound had occurred at least one hour after death. Tsuda could not, therefore, have killed Raffaella, nor witnessed her death— as she was seen alive shortly before ten, and Tsuda had been in the big hall until after two a.m.

And immediately after the telephone call, the now familiar throb which heralded the arrival of the police helicopter—this time spewing forth a man unique in the *commissario*'s experience, which was extensive. A youngish, dissipated face, ready to dissolve into roguishness. The face was green now, and the slight figure almost collapsed into the *commissario*'s arms. Albert Drayton, Tsuda's secretary. "Al."

"That . . ." he gestured at the whirring helicopter and shuddered. "On top of everything, on top of the shock of hearing about him, and catching the plane. I got the last seat on the nine o'clock from Paris last night. Then no sleep and the horrible identification at the mortuary, and the exhaustion of struggling with the language at the police station."

Inside, the *commissario* had Lucia bring him coffee, quite aware that what was really needed was alcohol.

"They insisted I come up here. At least you speak English. All my Italian seems to have fled with the shock. You haven't *any* idea why he was killed?"

"I'm hoping you can help. You've been his secretary a long time, you say."

"Over twenty years. I'd studied Japanese in Australia, and his father had extensive business there. I was hired originally to teach him English. When he opened a Paris office he put me in charge of it."

The *commissario* let him talk on.

"He was the soul of courtesy and delicacy. You should see his Paris apartment. A connoisseur with the money to indulge it."

"Why did he make this trip to Italy?"

"Oh, he came to buy a painting."

"What painting?"

"He didn't tell me. But he's been for years on the track of a good example of Venetian Renaissance."

"He collected paintings?"

"He was building up his private gallery in Tokyo. He has marvellous stuff. Many Italian artists."

"And who was he buying it from?"

Drayton turned bleary, innocent eyes on Gadda.

"He didn't tell me. He was all agog, though. Really excited at the thought of it. He had to come here in person. He wouldn't have anyone else come."

"Do you know when this was arranged and how?"

Drayton shook his head. "Probably when he was in Rome last month. My boss flitted round the landscape quite a lot. He probably saw the owner then."

"He often made purchases in Italy?"

"Oh, yes."

"Do you know a man called Renato Barbicinti?"

"No."

"Have a look at this." Gadda held out a copy of Tsuda's letter to the bank in Vienna.

"I never saw that." Drayton squinted at the letter. "He must have had it typed in Rome."

"Where would he do that?"

"At the Japanese Embassy perhaps. He knew the ambassador. He could have had one of the typists do it."

"Barbicinti told me Tsuda had arranged to have him bid at auctions here in Italy on his behalf."

Drayton shrugged.

"It could well be. He hadn't told me."

"Barbicinti could have found an original Venetian Renaissance painting for him. It might be what he came to get. Have you any idea *what* painting it could have been?"

Drayton said vaguely: "About eighteen months ago Tsuda made someone an offer for a Bellini Madonna. He got very excited about it, and then after all the owner wouldn't sell."

"A Bellini Madonna," said Gadda thoughtfully.

"Giovanni Bellini, you know," Drayton looked at him. "Not the father or brother."

"What?"

"I mean, Giovanni was one of the greats—a key figure in North Italian painting of the fifteenth century."

"Yes, all right," returned Gadda somewhat testily. "How much money was he intending to give for it?"

"I can't help you there. He kept a lot of things to himself."

"What hotel are you staying at?"

"The Hilton. I'm waiting on a call from Tsuda's wife. She'll be flying over with the son and daughter. It was a shocking thing to have to tell her over the telephone, as you can imagine."

"Mr. Tsuda was extremely rich?"

"Yes indeed."

Sensing that the interview was ending, Drayton rose and traced a slightly tottery path round the screen, the *commissario* on his heels. At the door he turned to Gadda and said:

"I'd like to have a look at those frescoes before I go. Tsuda must have been overjoyed to see them."

"Did you know he intended coming up here?"

"No. I had no idea what his movements were going to be here."

"Tsuda said the Japanese ambassador told him about the frescoes."

"It could be. They were known to one another."

"He's out of Rome. We can't check with him."

"That's so." Drayton shivered in the outside air and said gloomily: "Oh God, what am I going to do without him?"

XIX

Gadda went back to his table and rustled quickly through his notes. Then he called Doris Boot in. Doris showed signs of strain; her manner was jerky and her former great readiness to talk was gone.

"I went into the study just before the professor began his second lecture," she said guardedly, in answer to the *commissario*'s query. "Juliette had been in one time and raved afterwards about the lovely things Mowbray had there. So when I got a chance the next time the class met, I slipped in too, just to have a look."

"And you had a close look at the Bellini Madonna?"

Doris's eyes dropped briefly before Gadda's.

"Pretty close. It's a lovely painting. Such bright colours. You'd wonder how they stay so fresh after all that time. The blue in that dress of hers was almost too bright."

"What do you mean? The painting was a copy, wasn't it—presumably quite recently made?"

"Well of course, it would hardly be the real thing, would it?" Doris smiled furtively and darted a glance at Gadda. Then her eyes grew dull. "How could it be?" she asked, almost absently.

"What are you suggesting, Mrs. Boot?"

"Nothing. Nothing at all." Doris's mouth snapped shut on the words.

"There's nothing further you can tell me?"

"That I can't."

Muttering dismissal of Doris, the *commissario* left her abruptly and went to the ante-room to telephone.

"Please get Colombo on the job and take him along to the Mowbray apartment. Mowbray has a Bellini Madonna on the wall in his study. It's presumed to be a copy. It's . . . yes, it's worth following up. Can you get him there straight away? I'd be grateful. He is in Rome at the moment. Ah, that's fortunate. You'll phone me back then? No, you can get *him* to phone me directly from the Mowbray apartment."

He was left, in sick frustration, for the whole afternoon. The telephone was silent, the air cold and dead with oppression and anxiety. Most of the group had taken refuge in long walks, but by six o'clock a bridge table was going. Gadda noticed a good deal of drinking was taking place by the fire.

Just before dinner Mowbray appeared for the first time that day. At the precise moment that the *commissario* went to the kitchen for his own meal, the telephone rang.

"Yes, ah *yes*, Professore. Extremely obliging of you to . . . You speak from the apartment?"

It was Colombo, ex-director of one of Rome's most famous museums, and an authority on Renaissance painting. He had often been consulted in the past by the police on cases of thefts and forgeries of works of art.

"I may even say that I got there with all possible speed at the mere suggestion that a Bellini might have come to light!"

"And?"

"I may say that the Bellini Madonna in question is not the original."

"Ah. There is no question at all of it being so?"

"There is no possibility *whatsoever* of mistaking it for anything but a copy." The voice betrayed some amusement. "A rather competent, clever copy, but a copy none the less, and done a short while ago only on a modern canvas. To reproduce the light and colour of a Giovanni Bellini is scarcely an easy task. In fact, I cannot, I confess, quite understand why Dr. Mowbray, so well-known an authority, should have bothered to hang this painting above his desk, where his eyes must frequently rest on it. Why, indeed, he ever bothered to acquire it at all."

"You mean he would have done better to choose a reproduction?"

The telephone sighed, and laughed delicately.

"A reproduction!"

"If the copyist couldn't get the colours . . ."

"My dear Commissario, neither would the reproduction." The tone was reproving. "You see, a reproduction—especially of an artist such as Bellini—is *so* unsatisfactory. It is impossible, my dear Commissario, to re-create all the colours truly in a reproduction. You can choose the one you want and reproduce that, but the others will be wrong. It is not something we can do yet, you see, any more than we have found out how to cure the common cold!

"And Bellini's paintings were miracles of colour and light. You know, of course, this is the Borghese Madonna—one which was stolen over two years ago. A terrible loss. One of the very few Bellini in Rome. Quite irreplaceable. I would rather have had any other of his young women stolen. She is as young and as fair as any, peasant though she no doubt was. One of Bellini's attractions for me has always been the extreme youth of his Madonnas—they are mere children, most of them . . . But reproductions, Commissario . . ."

That laugh again, and the aloofness of the tone.

"There is only one way, Commissario, to look at paintings, and that is to go to the original. In this case, the frame in which the Bellini copy reposes—a fine one—is of more value than the painting."

"I am sincerely sorry to have bothered you, Professor. I must beg your forgiveness."

The voice permitted itself a further delicate tinkle.

"You need not. I would travel further than I did this morning on the chance of recovering a Bellini. I think, then, I cannot help you further, Commissario, er . . . er . . ."

Smarting, Gadda put down the telephone. But then he stood for a long while pondering. Something Colombo had said . . .

Another rapid traversal of the hall, without a side glance at anyone. Their eyes bored into his back. Gadda went outside and began a restless pacing up and down. Then he came inside once more.

"Tell Barbicinti I want to see him," he muttered to Dante. When Barbicinti appeared, Gadda said, rather morosely: "Sit down, if you please, and tell me this. You know Madame Deneuve reasonably well, is it not so?"

Renato's face, such a repository of expressions, betrayed surprise, irony, regret, all at once. He shrugged.

"She is one of my 'artists,' " he explained. "We meet on business mainly, though occasionally also for pleasure."

"Has she good, er, artistic judgement?"

Renato frowned.

"I don't think I quite understand. As a painter, she—"

"She must know quite a lot about paintings, old masters—"

"As a *painter*," Barbicinti's tone was derisive, "it does not follow. Not all artists bother with old masters."

"Would she know a good painting from a bad one?" asked the *commissario*, rather desperately.

Barbicinti's eyes narrowed.

"A good painting from a bad one . . ." he repeated slowly.

"Well, does she paint well herself?" interrupted the *commissario* rudely. "Does she know how to use colours and all that sort of thing?"

"*Ma sì*. She has a most advanced sense of colour in her own work. She is a most promising painter and some of her things are delightful."

"Signora Mowbray thought her stuff was rubbish."

Barbicinti's eyes filled with pain.

"You see," he explained, "Raffaella—many years ago—herself tried to paint." He laughed tragically. "She was no painter. But I suppose, living in Mowbray's world, she felt doubly outside of it for this reason, that she had tried and failed. I think she was jealous of Juliette's success."

"When she criticised Madame Deneuve's paintings in your gallery, were her comments valueless?"

"Let me say that what she said was in a way true, but that she was so busy pointing out defects that she entirely missed the merits, which were considerable. I would not otherwise have shown Madame Deneuve's work," added Renato fastidiously.

"It's no wonder Madame Deneuve was upset, then, especially as she missed a sale out of it."

Renato nodded.

"Yes. It's strange, really, that Raffaella had no real artistic judgement. But there . . ." He waved his hands, and his eyes filled with tears. "She was herself a painting . . ."

The *commissario* stiffened, staring at the other curiously.

"Va bene," he finally said. "What I want to know is this. Madame Deneuve would know an original old master from a fake, or a copy, rather?"

Barbicinti gained control of his face, all at once. His eyes shifted.

"I assure you . . . if the fake is a good one . . . some utterly amazing forgeries have been done. Even the experts—"

"No, no, you don't understand," grunted the *commissario*. "Would she confuse an original with a bad copy?"

"Might I ask . . . of which painter? And," Barbicinti's eyes narrowed, "with how bad a copy?"

"No, you mightn't." The *commissario*'s face reddened. "Can't you give a plain answer to a plain question for once? Is her judgement to be trusted in things artistic?"

"Oh yes." Barbicinti looked at the *commissario* with rather more respect. "She has a keen appreciation and a deep love of painting and is really rather well informed. Professor Mowbray would agree with me."

"Ask Madame Deneuve to come in, will you?"

She arrived, as usual, rather breathless, or at least looking so, her chest rising and falling rapidly. Her eyes showed alarm.

"I want you to do something for me."

"Yes?" She flushed right down to the collar of her black dress.

"I want you to go to Rome and have another look at that copy of Bellini's Madonna in Mowbray's study and tell me if it's the one you saw before."

"Go to *Rome!*" She might have been speaking of the North Pole.

"We'll lift you down by helicopter. You will then be brought straight back here."

Her eyes were bright and shrewd as she took in his words.

"What are you suggesting?" she burst out finally. "Why should it not be the same one?"

"On this point I have nothing to say," said the *commissario* smoothly. "You may ask, Madame Deneuve, but I shall not answer." His lips sucked in the final words and he was silent for a second or two.

Several possibilities occurred to Juliette, it was clear, each playing over her face in turn, for anyone to see.

The *commissario*, watching her, spoke again.

"You will go immediately, and you will telephone me from the Mowbray apartment. Do you understand, Madame?"

She opened her mouth to say a dozen things, but nothing came out. Finally she managed: "Never before do I ride in a helicopter."

"It is a very efficient means of travel. Fifty minutes will see you in Ciampino. A car will be waiting for you. Oh, I don't wish you to tell anyone here why you are going. There is no need, in fact, for them to know you are gone."

Juliette rose to her feet and looked with dignity down on the *commissario*.

"It is strictly necessary?" she asked.

He nodded. Without another word she turned on her heel and sailed around the screen, closely followed by the sergeant.

She was back within ten minutes wearing her coat and carrying her large carry-all for canvases.

"Commissario, you will allow me to visit my apartment and get some fresh clothes? It is close to the Mowbrays'. I am also expecting a letter which should be waiting for me. And I would take the opportunity to leave these two new paintings of mine in my apartment."

"Visit your apartment?" The *commissario* looked at her, pondering. "I'll need to check just what you have with you."

He inspected her handbag and the contents of the carry-all. It contained the Vicovaro scene he had already admired and a painting of a purple mountain seen through a Gothic window.

"They told me you are selling this one to Signor Van Dam. I saw it in his room."

"They both need finishing touches and finally some fixative," said Juliette. She was quivering at the prospect of the helicopter.

"This one of the mountain you have done up here? You work fast, Madame."

He escorted her to the helicopter himself and helped her in. He left her waiting in it while he returned and made a telephone call. Then he gave lengthy and explicit instructions to the sergeant, who was to accompany her.

He watched the helicopter take off, and then walked slowly back, his head down. Inside, he went straight to the ante-room, closed the door carefully, and talked at great length to his chief in Rome.

That night, no one welcomed the onset of darkness.

"Much more and I'll really go mad." Marjorie Bennett, usually placid, clutched Lady Loftus, who patted her as consolingly as she could. Two days had produced fresh lines and a pallor in Lady Loftus's face. She looked smaller and older.

"*You*'re so brave . . ." Marjorie felt compunction at her own outburst.

"I try to be," returned Lady Loftus. "It's not knowing who is . . . who is the enemy."

"Exactly!"

In her bedroom, Beverley sat with Hedda on the bed, talking little by now. They were drinking John Backhouse's Scotch whisky, nicely calculated to last them till dinner, and both were slightly drunk.

John Backhouse, by the light of a hurricane lamp, tried to read.

Van Dam, Jo Ann, Barbicinti and Doris played cards by the fire. Mowbray had walked for a long time and was now half asleep, over the other side of the hall, on his knees an open book which he had not even glanced at.

"Juliette *still* on that painting?" Jo Ann glanced abstractedly at the cards and, unknown practice for her, broke her opponents' concentration.

"She finished it ages ago." Doris grimaced as she got Van Dam's cigarette fumes full in her face.

"You going to buy that painting, André?" Jo Ann's fear made her sound sharp.

"I think so. Quite daring in conception. All that purple mountain seen through the window, and the white of the walls." Van Dam looked as concentrated and grim as a man about to run a marathon. He pulled hard on his cigarette and again the fumes attacked Doris.

"You've changed your brand, I see," said Doris bad-temperedly. "Much less strong what you're smoking now, which is fortunate when someone else gets the smoke full in their face!"

"Sorry. They're Jo Ann's," muttered Van Dam. "I ran out."

"Caporal you smoked before, wasn't it?" asked Doris.

"What? Yes, Caporal."

"I thought so. You can't mistake *that* smell. Juliette's car still reeks of them, d'you know that? All this time after you were in it, too."

"Do you really not know where Juliette is?" burst out Barbicinti suddenly. He sounded at the end of his tether.

At that moment the helicopter roared above them. Everyone jumped.

"Bother Juliette. André, it's your bid," said Jo Ann sternly. So long as she was in company with all the others, she felt reasonably brave. She felt she contributed calm common sense. The very sound of her own voice, full of reason and moderation, made her feel better. It was only when she had to walk down that corridor at night and go to bed that good sense and reason took to the winds, blotted out perhaps by ghosts of monks long since laid to rest.

Even now, as it happened, Juliette was confronting the *commissario* on the terrace outside. He had been waiting for her.

"There is no doubt. It is the same painting." Her tone was decided.

"I see. You know, I had the idea it might have been a painting of considerable value. I hear from Mrs. Boot that you were extremely impressed with it when you first chanced to see it."

"Ah," Juliette was vehement. "*She* does not know paintings. It is a beautiful painting, but not of course to be compared with Bellini's own work, I imagine!" She laughed gently.

"The original was stolen," said the *commissario*, falling into step with her and holding open the big door into the main hall.

"Yes, so it was. A terrible thing."

"Thank you, Madame Deneuve. It was a stray idea of mine that had no issue."

He smiled at her so suddenly that she was a little flustered, since it was a smile that attempted charm. And she even bridled somewhat as together they entered the main hall.

"I suppose there's no reason why we shouldn't go to bed," Lady Loftus said much later. Her face was haggard. "It's getting on for midnight."

"I feel bored as well as frightened now," said Jo Ann frankly. "And I also will just scream if something doesn't happen. This waiting."

"Juliette's got Mowbray talking at last," commented Doris, glancing at the pair on the far side of the fire. "He looks a better colour."

They kept glancing anxiously at the screen down the other end of the hall, and whenever a police officer appeared, whenever the telephone rang, a quiver of restlessness passed through them.

Beverley and Hedda had not been seen for some time, but now, aloof and withdrawn, they sought the warmth of the fire.

"You might give us the latest," said Doris, glancing quickly at them. Her eyes dropped once more to the book on her knees. "You were the last to get the third degree. Old *commissario* getting anywhere yet?"

Beverley's eyes travelled many miles down from the ceiling to focus on Doris and she said:

"What?"

"I said is the old *commissario* getting anywhere?"

Beverley's eyes suddenly blazed.

"He should, with *your* help," she said bitterly. "There can't be much he doesn't know about every one of us by now."

"I don't know that I care much for that remark." Doris's mouth snapped shut on the words and she looked balefully at Beverley.

"You told him something about Hedda," said Beverley, evenly and ominously.

Doris raised her eyebrows and gave a tiny shrug.

"I'm sorry," she said spitefully, "if there was some reason to hide *facts.* You should have said so . . ."

Very ostentatiously she gave her attention once more to her book.

"You miserable specimen of humanity, with your filthy little bird-brain and your disgusting little snippets of information!" All Beverley's fear and tension found expression in anger. "Why in God's name did you ever come up here? Just to find meat for gossip?"

"Steady on, Beverley." A large hand gripped Beverley's shoulder from behind and John Backhouse pushed her down into her chair. Then his eyes swept over Doris. "There's no doubt some people talk too much and too misleadingly, however." His voice cut like a whiplash.

"I've never been insulted like this in my life." Doris spoke the words with tight lips and her little eyes glistened. Her fingers tore at her red neck-scarf. With an unwonted surrender to nerves, she pulled it off and threw it down. Then, with an attempt at composure, she grasped the book she had been looking at and turned on her heel. Head in air, she stalked over to the other side of the hall, where Mowbray and Juliette still talked.

"I thought you might like a look at this, Dr. Mowbray." Doris laid the great tome down in front of him. "It belongs to Marjorie. She found it in a second-hand shop in Subiaco and she's rather taken with it."

"A fine production indeed." Mowbray bent abstractedly over the lavishly illustrated history of Italian painting.

"It's got lovely reproductions of the Venetian painters," pointed out Doris. "We all hope you'll lecture on them one day, Dr. Mowbray . . ." She paused for a moment, checked that Beverley was watching her, and continued. "There's certainly a lot to look at in paintings, isn't there? I used to think a lot of them were quite ugly, like those dreadful ones of Christ on the cross. But I was thinking about what you were saying the other day, how a painting should tell you something . . ."

Doris droned on, shooting a triumphant look in Beverley's direction every so often. Juliette, yawning a little, lay back in her chair and closed her eyes.

"I'd like to ask you one thing," continued Doris, lowering her voice. "I'm not saying I know much about art, but a person can learn, I suppose. Would you say Mrs. Backhouse was so well informed—on painting, I mean?"

She fixed her bright, hard little eyes on Mowbray, who raised his brows in astonishment.

"Well now, how can I answer that?" His tone was perplexed. "Let's say I hope she's better informed now than at the beginning of the lecture course." He laughed mirthlessly and left Doris to digest his words.

Doris nodded her head, wisely.

"I thought so," she said secretively. "Of course, some people are such know-alls and can't bear anyone else to have a say . . ." She paused, and then said, "I'm really looking forward to hearing about the Venetians. I've been reading about them in advance."

"Yes?" There was irony in the tragic old eyes of the art historian. He glanced at Juliette, but her eyes had closed.

"Yes," pursued Doris. "Tintoretto and so on. Tell me, Dr. Mowbray, is Bellini your favourite painter?"

Was Doris talking for enjoyment's sake, because she felt sorry for him, or because she wished to taunt Beverley Backhouse? Or was she playing a deeper game? Mowbray didn't know. What was she saying now? He concentrated with an effort on her words.

"My favourite painter?" he sighed. "Not Giovanni Bellini really. A pupil of his, Tiziano."

"Titian? Now what was it about him?" Doris screwed up her eyes, in an effort to remember.

"Una verità stupenda, capace di dire tutto! I quote Goethe." Mowbray smiled faintly.

"Well, I haven't got up to him yet."

"Nor ever will, Madame . . ." muttered Mowbray, a little wildly.

"I'm getting fond of Bellini," Doris insisted. "I've been studying him mainly because that painting you have was the first real Italian painting I ever saw." Doris paused.

Mowbray said nothing. He looked over at Juliette, as if for support, but Juliette had dozed off.

"I do admire that one in your study," pursued Doris. "In fact, you have two of them, haven't you? There was another one on the floor, propped up against the wall, that time I peeped in . . ." After a moment, she added: "Sometimes you wonder who the artist's model was." Doris met Mowbray's eyes. "Someone said Bellini used peasant women quite a lot. Perhaps *she* was a peasant."

Doris had been sitting on a low chair; she now sprang up and fell back a step. For Mowbray had suddenly come to life, his eyes blazing. He straightened up in his chair. But then, as suddenly, his head sagged forward on his chest and his eyes closed.

Doris relaxed. Tapping Juliette on the shoulder and startling her into wakefulness, she gave her a meaning look and tiptoed away to the other side of the hall, where Jo Ann was distributing coffee.

"No, I shan't have any," said Doris. "I'm going to find it hard enough to sleep as it is."

"You can have one of my sleep-pills, if you like," offered Jo Ann. "Put you out like a light."

"I don't think I'd like to take anything like that," Doris said doubtfully.

Beverley opened her mouth, looked at Doris, and then resolutely closed it again.

"I will give you some of my herbal mixture," said Juliette. "I have a spare packet or two. Get a jug of hot water from Lucia."

As they walked together along the corridor, Doris yawned.

"I feel so tired. Two nights without sleep now. Not a wink last night. I don't know why. I didn't take anything to make me sleep because of not having slept Saturday night either. Saturday it was all that strong drink and food. I was up and down to the bathroom all night. Embarrassing. Everyone else was sound asleep, anyway." Doris suddenly quavered. "All but the murderer." Suddenly, she came to a dead stop, her eyes wide. Juliette swung round enquiringly. "You know, I've only just remembered," continued Doris slowly. "The last time I got up, I suppose about four-thirty, I blundered into the wrong room— the one next to mine—André's, that is. And he wasn't there. Not a trace of him. And I can tell you, he wasn't in the bathroom, either!"

Doris paused at her own door, looking fearfully at Juliette. "Do you think I should tell the *commissario?*"

Juliette shrugged and pursed her lips thoughtfully.

"No, I wouldn't." She smiled and squeezed Doris's arm. "He is such a nice man and—he is buying my paintings! You don't want to get him arrested! Now stop your worrying and get to bed. I'll drop the *camomille* in to you in a few minutes, if I can find it."

Out in the big hall, a young policeman approached the group at the fire with a half-supercilious, half-respectful air.

"The *commissario* wishes to announce that the *signori* are at liberty to retire to bed."

They needed no encouragement. The men hung back for twenty minutes or so to allow the women to be clear of the bathroom. Then Mowbray went off first, John Backhouse, André Van Dam and Renato Barbicinti following.

More than one of the women, having pushed home the makeshift bolt inside her door, gave herself the added protection of a heavy chair against the door. To most, sleep came hard, once the hurricane lamps were extinguished or turned down.

Juliette, with trembling hands, searched her belongings for camomile. Beverley paced up and down her cell, stopping now and then to take a sip from a hip-flask. Hedda, fully clothed still, lay sprawled on her bed, smoking. Jo Ann, waiting for her sleeping-pill to work, wrote a letter to her son at school in California. Lady Loftus lay still under her blankets, prepared for sleep but unable to succumb as thoughts—terrible thoughts, resolutely suppressed in public—came rushing upon her now like wolves. Louise Parsons slept within twenty minutes, thanks to one of Jo Ann's sleeping-pills, while Marjorie Bennett stared into the blackness, saw the crumpled form of Raffaella and felt—yet again—the whole world lurch and tilt around her.

Charles Mowbray was at his table, deep in thought, his handsome face splendidly accentuated by the hurricane lamp, the fingers of one beautiful hand drumming nervously on the rough wood. Renato Barbicinti sat on his bed, head in hands. André Van Dam, grim of face, sat staring unseeing at the opposite wall. John Backhouse, who had no intention of sleeping yet, was writing at the rough wooden table, bottle and glass beside him, tonight very clear of head indeed.

Doris was also writing. Her fountain-pen scratched away energetically in a small diary which accompanied her everywhere. She finished a page and sat for a moment listening to the howling of the wind, feeling suddenly forlorn, possessed of a desperate longing to be in comfortably mundane surroundings. All this art business was all very well, but murders were too much. If only it were an ordinary morning in the apartment in Rome, and she was having a chat with a friend of hers, Edie Plummer, the wife of a British Embassy clerk, who lived above the Boots. Over a long-drawn-out cup of coffee Doris would tell her, not for the first time, how the *tuttofare* left her apartment looking clean, when it was not, and how she was by now quite certain that the woman stole money now and then; together, she and Edie would enjoyably pick over the deficiencies of life in Italy. Sighing, Doris hid the diary in her toilet bag.

A tap on her door startled Doris, but then she remembered the herbal mixture. Saying to herself, "That'll be Juliette," she hastened to pull back the chair from the door.

She shot back the sliver of wood and peered out into the darkness. Without coming into the room, Juliette thrust the little packet of camomile into Doris's hand, and said:

"Let it infuse for five minutes at least."

Doris took the packet and bolted her door once more. She dropped the packet into a mug and poured water over it from the steel hot-water jug Lucia had given her. She yawned, and sat down heavily on the bed. Five minutes . . .

Another tap on the door. Juliette *was* a fusser. Doris shot back the bolt and peered out once more. And this time, her red scarf —which she had left behind in the big hall—was dangled before her . . .

XX

The *commissario* said to Augusto: "Leave the door of the ante-room open when you go to bed. I'm expecting a call."

The call that never came. After all these hours . . . So, his hunch was wrong?

At one-thirty he woke Dante, who was to relieve the man on duty in the corridor outside the cells, Gadda's hope was to snatch some sleep himself. Dante couldn't stand being woken in the small hours. He drank down the coffee the *commissario* himself had brewed and strapped on his holster, departing in silence.

The *commissario*, alone in the big hall, felt reluctant to sleep. It was so late he was getting his second wind and his brain raced. Standing before the fire, his thoughts roved over the men and women now asleep in the cells.

Backhouse. He could have quarrelled with Raffaella on arrival. Doris Boot had found him plunged in gloom and even fury after dinner. A crime of ungovernable passion? He probably worked like a devil, with hardly any respite from the pressures of his job. What if he had killed her, got up early to hide the gun, been seen by Tsuda? If Tsuda had seen the body and accused Backhouse there and then?

Beverley Backhouse, who was going to lose her husband to Raffaella. Was she quite sane? These sick fancies, her apparently deadly hatred of Raffaella, fostered by her revolver practice, using a glossy photograph of Raffaella taken by Backhouse for a target! Backhouse thought her capable of it.

Hedda. Oh, she could murder. A crime of self-sacrifice. She had the nerve and the coolness and had—he was sure—already made a deliberate attempt in loosening the wheel of the Simca. Hedda: with the ash-blonde hair, the pale gold skin, that slightly brooding, slightly mocking exterior, the lazy grey eyes. She and Beverley: rich girls, beautiful spoilt rich girls with little slim hands, who wore their expensive clothes so carelessly.

Backhouse would protect them both—Beverley as his wife.

"M'wife . . ." My property! His insolent, impatient tone. Scandal wouldn't touch her. And his protection extended even to his wife's girl lover. Nothing was going to injure Backhouse's career.

There could be no connection with Tsuda. Tsuda had by chance stumbled on the truth next morning. It was the only explanation.

The *commissario* got up and roamed round the hall, head down, coming to a dead stop every so often. The chairs remained as their occupants had left them. Over there Juliette and Mowbray had talked by the fire. Here was a card table. Various objects were scattered round. A velvet jacket of Juliette's. A packet of American cigarettes, several books.

Gadda looked at the title of one of the books. *Italian Painters of the High Renaissance.* The author was C. W. B. Mowbray. A de-luxe edition. Expensive to produce, it would have a limited sale. The Mowbray bank account, he had been informed, showed a very moderate balance.

He settled down by the fire with the book. Inside the dust-cover, he read:

Professor Mowbray brings a singular level of critical appreciation to bear on his subject. His wit, his lightness of touch and deft manipulation of the English language make this book a sheer delight . . ."

On the back of the dust-cover was a short biography:

Born in 1925, Professor Mowbray was educated at Hurst Grammar School, near Reading. He spent the years 1944 and 1945 in the army, seeing active service in Italy, and attaining the rank of captain. After the war, he studied history at Cambridge, then spent two years in repertory in Shakespearean and old English comedy roles. Becoming increasingly interested in art, he finally devoted himself to art history and criticism. He has written nine books, the most widely read being *The Art of Giovanni Bellini* (1958) and *Venetian Painting of the Quattrocento* (1962). He has travelled extensively in Europe and the Near East and has resided in Italy for the past twenty years.

Why had Raffaella left the lecture? Headache or no, unac-countable. The lecture was important and she always worked the projector. Was it the only time she could be sure of seeing Backhouse alone?

In the darkness, most of them had hardly been aware of her departure. The *commissario* thought his head was not too clear any longer and he gave a great yawn. Doris Boot had come in, hadn't she, just after Raffaella left the hall. She would have met Raffaella coming out if Raffaella had headed towards the cells, down that long, long corridor. Doris had said nothing about meeting her, however.

The *commissario* sat up and rustled through his notes. Jo Ann's evidence. "About ten or fifteen minutes after the begin-ning of the lecture, Mrs. Mowbray left to go to bed. Then Doris came in . . . almost immediately. I know, because that draught was really icy, and no sooner had the door closed than it seemed it opened again and Doris slid into place at the end of the row."

Doris Boot. She must in that case have seen Raffaella before she entered the hall. Why had she not mentioned it? The *com-missario* got to his feet and instinctively made to shout for the sergeant, before he caught himself up. Could he disturb Doris now? His watch showed two-twenty a.m. He supposed he had better leave it till morning . . .

He sank down. He was suddenly utterly exhausted, his limbs like logs of wood, his eyes burning. A bunk awaited him in the ante-room. He'd get up in a moment and . . .

The *commissario*'s head dropped forward on his chest and in an instant he slept.

"Commissario, *buongiorno!*"

Lucia, clattering back and forth to the fire, which now blazed merrily, had been keeping a sharp eye on the snoring form of the *commissario*, who had slept where he had fallen six hours before. Her *"Buongiorno!"* fairly bellowed out, seemed to tweak every aching bone in his body. She gazed down on him with inquisitive black eyes, enjoying having an important mem-ber of the police force under her thumb for the moment.

"Lei ha dormito qui invece di andare a letto," she bawled.

Muttering imprecations, she bent over the fire. *"Oggi è" una bella giornata però'."* She had a great store of such commonplaces, which followed one upon the other without any necessarily logical sequence. Her voice was tremendous.

Gadda retreated to the wash-house off the kitchen and, standing before Augusto's shaving mirror, scraped off his whiskers. As he finished the phone rang, and he cut himself and swore and rushed to grab it himself. It was not the development he had hoped for, but this disclosure set his heart racing.

"Go and get Barbicinti," he said to Lucia. "In another twenty minutes, go and wake the others, Mrs. Boot first. I want to see her when I've finished with Barbicinti."

Lucia disappeared and the *commissario* watched Augusto going about his duties quietly and efficiently. A slight, compact, beautifully built man, withdrawn and grave of aspect. He came from Abruzzo, as did Gadda himself. He had been greatly taken with Raffaella, though he had known her for hours only.

"She was a *signora talmente gentile . . ."* he had said simply and with immense dignity. "She gave her orders like a highborn lady."

"You were not present at Saturday's lecture, I suppose?" asked the *commissario* now.

"Hardly! Lucia and I were listening to the radio by the stove here, after we finished the dishes."

"Ah, the radio which was heard by mistake in the cells that night?"

Augusto smiled faintly.

"You see, there is a hollow channel in the rock between this room and the old cells, which lie underneath it. From this precise point only" (he pointed to the bell) "does the sound carry—to all but the two end cells."

Was Italian better than English when it came to bullying someone? To worrying away at them? At least it was Gadda's native tongue.

"We've heard from the Bankhaus Aschenbach in Wien." Gadda's single statement greeted Barbicinti when he appeared. Taken first thing in the morning before coffee it shook Barbicinti to his depths.

"I told you before, he asked me to attend certain auctions
. . ." he stammered.

"What were you supposed to buy for him? The Colosseo?"

"Antiques cost the world nowadays."

"Eight hundred and fifty million lire! He put eight hundred
and fifty million into an account only you could draw on. You
could have gone to Wien the next day and drawn the lot. They
said so."

"Some things cost money, that's all."

"*What* things, for instance?"

"Well, Rubens's 'Samson and Delilah' was sold at a Christie's
auction the other day for about five *miliardi di lire.*"

"You were to buy a painting for him."

"I never said that."

The *commissario* suddenly grasped Barbicinti by the shoulder and pulled him to his feet.

"*E tutto quello che lei mi ha detto, vale un bel nulla!*" Gadda's
face practically touched Barbicinti's for a second in his rage.
"Tsuda came here to buy a painting. We know that. It was a
Bellini, wasn't it? That money was for a Bellini."

The single name seemed to bite into Barbicinti's face. The
commissario followed it up quickly.

"Tsuda came to Italy to buy a painting. You had a painting to
sell. You had a Bellini—a stolen Bellini. I'll arrest you now,
Signore, if I don't get the truth this minute. Arrest you for
murder."

"It wasn't mine." Barbicinti just managed to get the words
out. "I had no part in it."

"What!"

"He wanted to buy the Bellini Madonna. I never killed him. It
came as the biggest shock in the world to me. And as for Raffaella . . ."

"Who killed Raffaella?"

"God, I don't know! I tell you I don't know!"

"Talk!"

"The painting was Professor Mowbray's. It had been stolen.
How Mowbray got it I don't know. Tsuda, who had connections
all over the place, somehow heard about the Bellini Madonna
and made Mowbray an offer for it. He did it through one of his

own employees, not personally. Mowbray wouldn't sell. That was about two years ago. Recently, Tsuda tried again. He called up Mowbray himself in Rome. But Mowbray was away. He saw Raffaella, and she told him she would sell it."

"Without Mowbray's consent?"

"Without his knowing."

"He'd *have* to know."

"No. After Juliette Deneuve burst into his study, Mowbray hid the Bellini original. It was easy for him. There was a centuries-old secret compartment—a *cache*—in the wall of his study. No one who didn't know about it could have put a finger on it. Raffaella knew about it, of course. She simply removed the Bellini just before she came up here."

"And on the proceeds of the sale you were to get married, I suppose."

"Eventually. In the meantime, the money was safe and couldn't be traced to her."

"And it all went to you!"

Barbicinti, white faced, stared at the *commissario*.

"It was *her* idea! *Hers!* She wanted part in lire but she didn't dare have Tsuda pay the rest into an Italian bank for her. Mowbray would have found out. She asked him for fifty million in cash and for the bulk to be paid into an account in my name, and she decided on the Bankhaus Aschenbach in Vienna."

"Did Tsuda have the painting when he left here?"

"I suppose so. Raffaella handed it to him immediately we arrived here Saturday evening."

"What did he do with it?"

"It went straight into the boot of his car."

"So! And Mowbray found out."

"I don't know!"

"And took his revenge."

Barbicinti stared at Gadda fearfully.

"And then lay in wait for Tsuda—the only other who knew he had the painting. But why not you, Barbicinti? You knew too!"

"D'you think it hasn't occurred to me? D'you think I haven't been expecting hourly . . ."

"Or else," Gadda said grimly, "you're the biggest scoundrel I've ever encountered . . . who traded on the girl's affection for you to induce her to steal the Bellini and sell it. The account was made out in your name . . . And then you did for her, and the—"

"And killed the goose who laid the golden egg! Very likely!" Anger overcame the young man's fear. "I never knew she arranged for the money to go into a bank account for me. I swear it. Not until last Saturday night. She told me after Tsuda had already got the painting. If anything, I was annoyed!"

"Where's your proof that the painting was Mowbray's? It could have been yours. I wonder if it was. I wonder if *you* were selling it—and Raffaella objected! So you disposed of her, and quarrelled with Tsuda!"

"No, no!"

"Where's the painting now?"

"I tell you I don't know. I don't know what happened to it!" Barbicinti insisted. "It's disappeared into thin air."

The telephone shrilled. With a contemptuous look at Barbicinti, the *commissario* hurried off.

In the sleeping quarters, Lucia knocked on each door in turn, waited until a sleepy face appeared, and boomed out that breakfast was ready in the big hall.

Signora Boot's door gave at Lucia's touch, though the cell was in darkness. Perhaps she had gone to wash. From Van Dam's cell there was only a surly response to her knock. Signora Partridge had her hair in curlers. Signora Hardegen looked as beautiful as a dream in cascades of ivory silk. It seemed too bad to have to wake the old professor. He received her politely, however, unlike Signor Backhouse, who stared at her rather stupidly, as though he had never seen her before. At the end of the corridor Lucia poked her head into the bathroom, whisked a cloth round the washbasins and returned to Signora Boot's cell.

"Signora!" she called importantly. "Signora, *buon giorno!*"

Still receiving no reply, she groped her way into the room and across to the window, which she opened in order to manipulate the heavy wooden shutter. A thin shaft of watery light crept in, and Lucia turned towards the bed to regard the dark head on the pillow.

"Signora, scusi del disturbo, ma—"

Opening her mouth, Lucia let out the most terrible wail the monastery could ever have heard. But Doris heard nothing. She lay fully clothed under the bed-coverings, with purplish face, staring eyes and protruding tongue.

Last Act

XXI

"What is he doing in there? It is too much. How long do we sit here in suspense and ignorance?" Juliette demanded of the others. She was near to breaking point and the cup clattered in the saucer as she took coffee from a frightened Lucia.

"The helicopter has only just come with the police doctor." Lady Loftus was trying hard to be calm but the effort was painful to watch.

"I feel," gasped Juliette, "I feel I cannot endure more." She placed her hand on her heart. "I . . ." Her brown eyes took in the whole group. "I am afraid . . ."

"I don't feel too good myself," said Jo Ann abruptly.

They had been instructed to stay in the big hall. Beverley sat as close as she could to her husband, her eyes on Hedda, who paced up and down on her long beautiful legs.

"Poor little Doris," murmured Marjorie Bennett. "Only last night sitting in this very chair . . ." She shivered. ". . . and talking about painting."

"I think of her husband and her poor little children at school in England," said Lady Loftus, her voice breaking.

Juliette sprang up, her eyes wild. "There is a maniac amongst us."

"Steady on," said Van Dam, coming up silently behind her.

Juliette gave a great start and swung round, instinctively drawing back from him. "We do not know each other," she said impressively.

"I'd like to know just what you mean by that," Van Dam said grimly. "I think you must pull yourself together."

"It is too much now, too much!" Putting her head in her hands, Juliette gave way to sobs.

"Look, you'd better take one of these," said Jo Ann, holding out a packet of tablets. "It'll calm you down."

"What is it that you give me, I should like to know?"

"Tranquillisers—only mild ones," explained Jo Ann.

"You think any of us should receive to eat, to drink from any one other? You think that? In this dreadful, delicate situation?" Juliette palpitated.

"Well," said Jo Ann disgustedly, plumping down on a chair. "If you suspect me of trying to poison you, of course—"

"No, it is not so, do not think it," said Juliette pitifully. The tears coursed down her pink cheeks. "In any case, I am in full view of all of you assembled. It would be madness to try it."

With resolution, she accepted the glass of water which Louise had poured for her, and popped a tablet in her mouth.

"Well, good for you!" Jo Ann raised expressive eyes to heaven and, pointedly turning her back on Juliette, walked over to the fire.

Van Dam gave a snort of nervous laughter and went over to stand near Mowbray, who was talking to one of the policemen. Hedda, who had paused at Juliette's outburst, sat down and put her arm round Beverley. Lady Loftus, her lips trembling, fumbled in her large travelling handbag and brought out some needlework.

"It will keep me sane," she said, with an attempt at dignity.

In Doris's cell, the *commissario,* with a face like thunder, listened to the police doctor.

"Strangled with her own scarf about one a.m. or soon after, very soon after she returned to her room."

"Doesn't help much. They all went off together last night, just after midnight. And," added the *commissario* bitterly—for the benefit of the policeman who had been on duty the previous night up to the time Dante took over and who stood behind him —"no one heard a thing, of course."

"Signor Commissario," the man protested, "the cells are quite sound-proof and it was my job to circulate."

"It never occurred to you to check that all was well, when the door here was ajar?" the *commissario* snapped.

"I did not see it . . . I did not notice that it was ajar!"

Neither had Dante. Gadda turned an irate back to him and muttered:

"She opened the door to whoever it was, man or woman. Could have been a woman. And her murderer couldn't have bolted it again from outside. He could only pull it to." With the tip of a finger, Gadda turned over a page of a small book lying on the table. "She had already written up her diary for the day. Kept it in her toilet bag. Peculiar place for it."

"I'll let you have further findings, of course." The doctor was packing his bag. He glanced sympathetically at the *commissario*.

But Gadda was already deep in the diary. Doris had written up a lurid account of the last twenty-four hours which would have made the *commissario* smile if he had not been so appalled.

"Murder!" she had headed up last night's page:

I little thought I'd ever be interviewed by an Italian *commissario*. Just like a *giallo*. I was complimented on my intelligence and on being "unbiased." Beverley lay into me because I gave the *commissario* certain information; nerves getting her down, obviously. If I didn't have my own pet theory I'd be inclined to suspect one of the Backhouses of doing the poor *girl* in (although she almost deserved it, carrying on with a married man and playing him off against B).

Gadda sighed impatiently as he screwed up his eyes to decipher the cramped writing. *"Che Dio ci aiuti,"* he muttered.

Someone would mourn Doris, and he felt a passing anger at the thought of her two young children, though anger different from that which had gripped him at the death of Raffaella. His eyes skimmed the preceding pages. Beverley had been "unspeakable," Hedda "horrid." He might leave the diary till later. Then he stiffened and gave the book absolute attention.

"You gave Doris Boot some *camomilla*. A glassful was untouched in her room." The *commissario* accused Juliette, who
sat like a ramrod before him, bright colour in both her cheeks.

"And it is *all* I did!" Juliette's voice trembled.

"Afterwards?" asked Gadda sternly.

"I went directly to bed. I was tired, tired." Juliette began
talking rapidly. "I had had as much as I could suffer at that
time . . ."

"All right." Gadda looked at his notebook. "Turn your mind
back to Saturday night and Mrs. Mowbray leaving the lecture.
Can you recall just how long afterwards Doris Boot came in?"

Juliette's fingers played incessantly with her pearls.

"She came in almost immediately. I remember, as she took
the chair next to me."

"Almost immediately. As much as five minutes after?"

Juliette frowned. "Not more than one or two minutes, I think.
Dr. Mowbray had begun to speak again after his wife went out.
When Doris came in he sounded annoyed at another interruption. And then Doris talked in whispers while she was settling
herself. Then," pursued Juliette, who was as usual finding relief
from tension in speech, "later, towards the end of the lecture,
she dropped off to sleep, and Dr. Mowbray lit some candles near
him and came to his finale, very dramatic it was you understand, and he sees that Doris is sleeping, and he says to her, "Ah,
aha, you are resting, Madame! But you should not be so!" It is a
little mean of him, you see, but he seeks very much the effect
. . . he—"

"He was an actor in his youth. Professional."

"This I know." Juliette nodded distractedly, never ceasing to
talk. "He must have been marvellous, marvellous . . ."

"Dr. Mowbray!" Gadda's manner had changed perceptibly and
he was now abrupt, even rude. "How much time passed after
the departure of your wife and the entrance of Mrs. Boot?"

Dr. Mowbray waved a vague hand, standing looking down on
Gadda.

"I really cannot remember. A few minutes—three or four
minutes, perhaps. I do remember Mrs. Boot annoyed me very
much coming in so late. And then proceeding to snore through

the lecture. A pathetic little woman, as full of malice as a snake of venom. And," added Mowbray, "she wrote me an anonymous letter."

"No," said Gadda shortly. "She didn't. That letter was typed on a machine belonging to Hedda Hardegen."

"Is that so? I was wrong then. All the same, Mrs. Boot was a poor creature, as pathetically lacking in brain power as she was in artistic sense—lost, blind to the virtues and truths of life as she was to beauty."

The *commissario*'s senses reeled. "She was a human being," he snapped. "And has now been done to death."

"Ah yes, poor soul," sighed Mowbray, with utter indifference.

XXII

Was the *commissario* playing by intention on their nerves? He went back and forth from the ante-room telephone to his table behind the screen. The men and women by the fire might not have existed for him. The atmosphere was supercharged when, towards eleven—just in time to avert an explosion—he addressed them.

"Go to your rooms, all of you." He spat the words at them angrily. "Secure your doors and stay there till I call you. Augusto will ring the bells, which will sound in your rooms as they did centuries ago, or so I am told." His lips curled. "The Angelus!"

It was well after twelve, however, when the bells summoned them. They trooped out to a big hall arranged as it had been on Saturday night, the screen, projector and chairs all in place.

"Take the seats you had the other night." The *commissario*'s face was impassive. "Augusto, stay here," he added, to the dark little manservant. "No, wait. Dr. Mowbray is not here. Go and call him."

The *commissario* waited in dead silence, staring straight in front of him. Mowbray appeared at last and, disconcerted, said: "I must have dropped off to sleep."

"No matter," replied Gadda. "Take a chair, sir." He was

young, stern and very concentrated, leaning forward belliger-ently now to his audience. "You are an artistic group. Perhaps you won't be surprised to know that the key to these tragic events should be a work of art."

Murmurs of surprise broke the packed silence.

"We have found out some facts. First, Mr. Tsuda came to Italy from Paris to buy a painting." The *commissario* paused. "He came to Italy to buy a Bellini Madonna—the Bellini Madonna which was stolen from the Galleria Borghese in Rome two and a half years ago and which was acquired by Professor Mowbray."

The rapt silence following this announcement was shattered by Mowbray's loud, shocked laugh.

"Commissario! You are wrong—terribly wrong. Are you re-ferring to the Madonna hanging in my study in my Rome apart-ment? A copy—a clever *copy!*"

The *commissario* said harshly:

"I am not speaking of the copy you have at home, Professor; I am speaking of the stolen original."

"You are asserting that I called Tsuda up here—a man I had never set eyes on before—to buy a painting I never owned!"

"No, sir. Your wife did. Unknown to you, she was selling it to him. She was to hand the painting over to him up here."

"Tsuda—a connoisseur!" Mowbray was incredulous. "A con-noisseur buying a copy!"

"A connoisseur doesn't pay what he did for a copy." Gadda's voice was acid. "The sum agreed on was nine hundred million lire—or half a million dollars." He paused, then said succinctly: "The method of payment was this. Tsuda arranged with the Bankhaus Aschenbach in Vienna to pay this sum into a num-bered account to be drawn on by Signor Renato Barbicinti."

Noisy exclamations burst from his audience, and Gadda held up a hand for silence.

"These are all solid, proven facts," he insisted. "And Signor Barbicinti has admitted his part. Yesterday Tsuda's private sec-retary turned up. A Mr. Drayton, who manages his Paris office. Drayton told me that Tsuda had a magnificent private collec-tion of European painting in Tokyo. As Drayton said, Tsuda cared for the beauty of paintings, not their provenance. For years Tsuda had been searching for an example of the Venetian school. According to Barbicinti, Tsuda heard about two years ago that the Borghese Bellini was in Mowbray's possession and he instructed someone to make an offer for it on his behalf. Tsuda was willing to pay a phenomenal sum of money. Professor Mowbray wouldn't sell. But some weeks ago Raffaella Mowbray agreed to sell the Bellini to Tsuda without her husband's knowledge."

Mowbray raised his head and his voice rang out bitterly.

"May I ask you where this famous original is now?"

Gadda, with an exultant note in his voice, said as casually as he could:

"Oh, it's right here."

He motioned to the sergeant, who propped up on the table an oblong shrouded in cloth. Gadda drew half the cloth aside to reveal the Bambino seated, a plump and grave Bambino, with glowing porcelain skin. The Madonna remained shrouded by the cloth.

Mowbray sprang to his feet and crouched over the painting.

"Where did you get this?" His voice was strangled.

"In the cleverest of hiding-places." The *commissario* pulled the cloth back further to reveal a vista of bold purple mountains and white walls. "You see it has been painted over," he said, "and only about a quarter of the original has been uncovered so far, even though experts were at work all last night."

Mowbray straightened his back and turned away from Gadda, so the others had a view of his face. Something had gone out of it, to leave an unfamiliar expression. "As though," Jo Ann said later, "he was all by himself and no one else there and he'd . . . he'd stopped *acting*. And it was *awful*."

Someone said now in loud, scandalised tones: "Juliette's painting!"

"Just so." The *commissario*'s eyes were on Juliette now, as she sat trembling, her hand on her heart. "Yesterday I sent you to Rome, Madame Deneuve. You saw your chance to remove the real Bellini to a place of safety. But this was a fatal slip, for you made me suspicious. Why this urgency to get these two paintings of yours to Rome—one done in Vicovaro, the other done from your window up here? I had your telephone tapped before you got to your Rome apartment," he said softly. "And indeed you did telephone someone when you got there."

Juliette said nothing. She stared at him stupidly, all the rosy colour gone from her cheeks.

"You called the Mowbrays' maid, Elena Crispoldi. You told her to go to your apartment and to take your painting of the purple mountains straight to a certain gentleman who lives off the Via Veneto. Our men had only to wait for Crispoldi to reach your apartment. She had a key to your place and entered without trouble. After she left, we followed her." The *commissario's* face betrayed pride. "And we succeeded in arresting a man who is . . . very valuable to our investigation. And the maid as well, of course."

"At police headquarters, the woman was persuaded to talk. You all know the Palazzo Doria, that massive fifteenth-century edifice with walls four feet thick, heavily barred windows, iron grilles, its maze of long corridors, its well-manned porters' office. Almost impregnable. You needed help from inside. The maid admits that she passed on information and admitted you to Mowbray's apartment on several occasions. You paid her well. However, the study was always well locked and bolted. The maid herself was only allowed in to clean once a week."

Gadda was perambulating now, with every appearance of enjoyment, stopping in front of Juliette at nicely calculated intervals.

"At last you managed to get into the study and identify the Bellini, Madame. We have, by the way, been in touch with the Brera, Milan, where you worked for years as a professional restorer of old paintings. While you were there, a minor work disappeared in mysterious circumstances. Nothing could be proved against you. Of course, you paint charmingly yourself, but not well enough to live on the proceeds."

Juliette's head was bowed now. Gadda shrugged and turned to the others.

"So," he gave a wolfish grin, "in the search for a murderer, a stolen Bellini comes to light. A Bellini stolen three times over—first from the Galleria Borghese, secondly from Professor Mowbray by his wife, thirdly from Mr. Tsuda."

His eyes raked them. Mowbray sat motionless in his chair, a

slight smile still frozen on his face. But his eyes were focused on things or time far off. Juliette was alone and isolated in the midst of them all, her face blotched and tormented.

"As a result of the last two thefts," continued Gadda, "Barbicinti got the money, Juliette got the painting."

XXIII

"Murders!" hissed the *commissario*, with one of his telling grimaces. "Tsuda first. He was killed for the Bellini, of course. As soon as Barbicinti and Raffaella Mowbray got here at six o'clock Saturday evening, they handed the Bellini Madonna to Tsuda, and Barbicinti says Tsuda locked it in the boot of his Mercedes. The boot has a first-class lock and the Mercedes had only to be touched for a powerful burglar-alarm to sound.

"You all knew Tsuda planned to leave around five a.m. Sunday. Someone went down to the parked cars and lay in wait for him. There was a struggle. Tsuda's glasses were found on the ground trodden underfoot. Tsuda was killed, dumped in the Mercedes, and the killer drove it off. In that car, Rome was at most a couple of hours away. No one here would have known or suspected a thing. Everyone else was due to leave about nine or so anyway. The killer could have driven to Rome and caught a plane out. If he simply left Tsuda in his own boot, the body could have gone undetected for days, even weeks. In the car-park at Fiumicino airport, for instance.

"One thing ruined this simple plan. The landslide. We know now it occurred during the early hours of the morning. Up here you knew nothing of it. The killer was the first to encounter it—with the Bellini and Tsuda's body on board. A disaster. There was no cover for the Mercedes. Otherwise, Tsuda's departure might still have been simulated. The killer decided to stage an accident. Tsuda was put in the driving seat of the car and sent over the side of the cliff. It was hoped the car would burn, and reconstruction of the accident would be very difficult. The second stroke of ill luck was that the Mercedes got caught up and came to rest against a tree. Impossible to move it.

"The killer was forced back to San Donato. With the Bellini."
Gadda walked up to Juliette and gave her an ironical glance.
"A hiding-place had already been prepared for it, well in
advance."

Juliette, brilliant-eyed, stared at him hypnotised.

"The Bellini," continued Gadda, "fitted *precisely* into the
back of a canvas which Madame Deneuve painted in Vicovaro.
You all saw her do it, I think. A charming painting of the countryside. The Bellini could not be rolled up for fear of damaging
the paint. It had to be protected. And all through, according to
our experts in Rome, it has suffered no damage—not then,
when she secreted it behind her own Vicovaro painting, nor
even later, when she painted over it. The Bellini was," and for
the first time the *commissario*'s face relaxed and he gave Juliette an evil smile, "in highly competent hands."

The *commissario* turned his back on her suddenly and strode
up and down.

"Later that Sunday morning, Raffaella Mowbray's body was
discovered. Her death brought the police on the scene within
hours. The painting stayed behind Juliette's own Vicovaro canvas all Sunday. Not in Juliette's room, but in the room of Mr. Van
Dam, who had arranged to buy Juliette's own painting. I know
this, because Signor Barbicinti saw it there. In fact, Mr. Van
Dam caught Barbicinti going through his room and was very
angry. Mr. Van Dam was even in the room most of Sunday,
trying to sleep off a heavy cold."

"The Bellini was hidden behind Juliette's own canvas all this
time!" exclaimed Van Dam.

This amused the *commissario*. He laughed, roughly.

"Exactly. Juliette was worried about it, though. She thought it
too risky to leave it simply secreted behind another canvas. She
decided to superimpose a painting of her own on the Bellini
canvas. Yesterday, in the privacy of her own room, she painted
over the Madonna with this view from her window." Gadda
bent over the Madonna for a moment before turning back to
Juliette. "A pity for you you didn't leave it at that. What a clever
artist you are and how much thought and care went into your
plans for the Madonna . . ."

Gadda paused and they watched him transfixed. Then his lips drew back from his teeth and he said:

"Barbicinti got the money, Juliette got the painting. And three people met their deaths." He swung round and presented his back to them, head down, then as abruptly wheeled to face Juliette once more.

"So you collaborated, did you, you and Barbicinti? Two cold-blooded scoundrels, closely connected by your jobs. Moving in artistic circles. You learn that Mowbray has the Bellini Madonna. You want it. But the Palazzo Doria is like a fortress. It won't be easy. Then one day, at Barbicinti's gallery, Raffaella Mowbray appears—quite by chance. And Barbicinti is *delighted* to see her—for the first time for years. There are further meetings. He finds she still cares for him. He persuades her to run away with him. He is a terribly plausible and engaging liar, as I have found out. Raffaella tells him about Tsuda's offer. He persuades her to steal the Bellini and sell it to Tsuda. He persuades her to have Tsuda pay the money into an account in his name. And to hand it to him up here, because Barbicinti's plan goes further still." Gadda turned his face to the others. "They want a lot, he and Juliette. Not only the painting, but the proceeds too."

Suddenly Barbicinti was on his feet, white-faced, defiant, proud, strikingly handsome.

"I am guilty of nothing but yielding to Raffaella! *She* stole the Madonna! She it was who arranged with Tsuda for the money to go into an account in my name! My only crime is that I allowed it! And I knew nothing of Juliette's part in all this. I swear it."

"So, Madame!" Gadda gazed at Juliette. "You planned it alone, did you?" He added, cruelly: "A pity your plan included the death of poor Tsuda."

"No, no . . ." Juliette sprang up, clutching her throat. "You cannot think I did this. Not murder. I know nothing of any murder. Nothing!"

"I don't believe you, Madame." Gadda went up to her, his face savage. "I think you are a deliberate and cold-blooded killer. There is the direct evidence of the Madonna. The evidence of the maid. You could have handled a gun. You could have used that same gun to kill Tsuda."

"Doris. A woman, she does not strangle—" Juliette was ashen and terrified.

"She was strangled with her own scarf," Gadda snarled. "There is no death penalty even for multiple murders. But fifteen or eighteen years in an Italian gaol and you won't feel so good when you get out at about sixty years of age, Madame. There'll be no extenuating circumstances." His voice rose, then abruptly fell, and he added softly and insinuatingly: "Unless, of course, you want to tell the whole truth—just as it happened. You would then be protected and you would get a lighter sentence. You might be thought . . . commercial, rather than wicked."

Juliette raised a stricken face to him.

"*Never* have I killed. I could not have killed Tsuda. You have the word of Van Dam that all that night—all Saturday night—"

"*Not* his word. Your own. I am quite aware that you informed me, amid many blushes, that you spent the night in his room." Gadda turned to Van Dam. "Is it true?"

Van Dam ran a hand through his fair hair and shrugged.

"I fear *not*, Commissario."

"Ah, you fear *not*." Gadda regarded him calmly, then looked at Juliette. "So, Madame Deneuve, you are lying, yet again."

Juliette uttered a strangled cry.

"I will not be accused, and wrongly! He made me say so. He made me tell you I was in his room! All night in his room!"

"Oh come!" Van Dam laughed scornfully.

"He agreed to alibi you?" demanded Gadda.

"He made *me* alibi *him!*"

"You mean, Madame Deneuve, that Mr. Van Dam was not in his room, but elsewhere?" The *commissario* turned with sudden deadliness to Van Dam.

"He was in my car . . ." shrieked Juliette suddenly. "Waiting for Tsuda. He asked Tsuda for a lift back to Rome. The Japanese was immediately suspicious. He made excuses. He said he wasn't going to Rome, but to Milan. André tried to overpower Tsuda. Tsuda fought like a madman. André hit him. Tsuda died from it. His heart failed."

"I see. And a dead Japanese had to be disposed of," said the

commissario pleasantly. "Not easy for a woman, if we substitute
Madame Deneuve for Van Dam. Though not impossible."

"I am innocent!" Juliette was on her feet now, measuring up
fairly to the *commissario*. "I am innocent of murder. I had one
part and that was to identify the Bellini. To help—as a consul-
tant and artist. I never killed. Never, never! It was André Van
Dam. Only him."

"You believe this woman?" Van Dam's body was straining his
jacket to breaking point. "Are these shock tactics, Commissario? Where's your proof?"

"I've got proof," snapped Gadda. From his pocket he drew a
little book. "I have a silent witness. The diary of Doris Boot." He
turned pages and read out:

"Saturday. A dreadful night. All that wine. What a head.
Kept me awake, tired as I was. Tummy trouble too. Up and
down to the bathroom. First time about three. Went barg-
ing into the wrong room coming back. I shone my torch
before I realised I was in the room next door to mine—
André Van Dam's. Luckily he wasn't there . . ."

"What the hell does that prove?" exploded Van Dam. He rose
to his feet belligerently. "The woman got flustered and made a
mistake. There were other empty rooms. There is no proof, only
Juliette's quaverings. And what a witness *she*'d make—a common thief."

Gadda cut him short.

"Again." He referred still to the diary. "The entry for Sunday
night:

"Juliette's car was reeking of Caporals. André must have
been smoking there for hours. Ash on the floor. Why would
he have sat in a cold car all afternoon? Was he in the car
Saturday night instead, smoking to keep warm?"

Gadda turned to Juliette. "Were you working together?"
She gestured. "I told you. My part was only to identify the
Bellini. He . . ." She shot a terrified look at Van Dam.
"Well?"
"He was to get hold of it."
"I think," interrupted Van Dam peremptorily, "you will find

my credentials in order. I represent the Barrington Lett Galleries . . ."

"Yes, yes," replied Gadda impatiently. "You are the genuine representative of a genuine firm. A good cover for your other operations."

Van Dam frowned.

"This is crazy," he declared.

"A coincidence, I suppose, that an airline ticket for a Qantas flight leaving Rome six p.m. Sunday was found in your hotel room in Rome, together with your belongings neatly packed up ready for instant departure?"

"That proves nothing!"

The *commissario* said contemptuously: "You're forgetting Morante. You're forgetting him—the man we pulled in yesterday. He talked, and not only about Juliette. Now," the *commissario* angrily cut through Van Dam's protest, "sit down and shut up!" He turned to Juliette. "You sent the maid to Morante, an Italo-Australian. Is he the head of the gang?"

"I do not know," stammered Juliette. "I had my instructions from him. He has twice come to Rome to give me consulting work."

"Morante is a member of a syndicate with a base in Sydney," stated Gadda. "As you very well know. A syndicate dealing in faked and stolen art treasures. They sell stolen paintings, particularly in Asia."

Juliette hung her head. "I had only to advise him," she whispered.

"They sent Van Dam to Rome to do the dirty work?"

"To get the Madonna. The study was always locked. The maid was allowed in once a week to clean, but only when Mowbray was present. But first I had to get in to identify the Madonna. I suggested that André should try to join Mowbray's class."

"To spy out the land?"

"Yes, and to find a way of getting me inside the study."

Gadda singled out Beverley and asked:

"Were you in this as well? You brought Van Dam up here."

"No, no," Juliette interrupted, distractedly. "Beverley met him because of me. I did not wish to introduce André myself to

Mowbray. I arranged a meeting between André and Beverley at my exhibition."

"Ah yes, when Raffaella Mowbray poured scorn on your paintings."

Something quivered on Juliette's face, flared and then died. She attempted a shrug.

"At the very first lecture, that is, before André joined the class, I managed to get into the study and saw the Madonna. It was unmistakably the original Bellini. Then, after the second lecture, I had a big surprise. *Doris Boot* told me she had actually gone into Mowbray's study. I had mentioned to her the beautiful things Mowbray had there and Doris was very inquisitive. Mowbray had forgotten to lock the study door when he came out to begin his lecture and Doris had slipped in. He found her, but not before she had seen two Madonnas, one of them on the floor leaning against the wall."

"Go on."

"Soon after, the maid Elena told me she thought the Bellini Madonna had been removed and had been replaced by a copy. She also told me Raffaella Mowbray received a visitor one day while the professor was out—a Japanese visitor. Elena overheard part of their conversation, which took place in Mowbray's study. She was sure that Raffaella was selling the Madonna to this man. Finally, she discovered that the Madonna was to change hands up here."

"How?"

"A letter came from Tsuda. For Raffaella Mowbray. It said Tsuda would be here at six p.m. on Saturday night. Elena found the letter in Raffaella's desk. She kept a close watch on Raffaella's mail after she found she was in communication with this man. And she knew English."

"A rare stroke of luck for you," commented Gadda. "Raffaella Mowbray did your work for you. Van Dam had only to choose his moment." He turned to the diary once more and read out:

"Monday. A terrible day. Tension and suspicion. Juliette working away like crazy at a new painting in her room. View through window she says. She won't let me see it. Why? It is unfair. She didn't mind in Vicovaro. I went in once when she had popped out for a minute. There was only a blank canvas. But when I saw it wasn't a new one. It was all painted over with some white coating and you could see the faint outlines of a painting underneath. Then Juliette came in and went for me in a real fury. Quite mad she was. Nerves, I expect.

Gadda paused and barked:

"Did she know what you were doing, Madame? Did she?"

Juliette sat transfixed, shaking her head vaguely as though in a dream.

"*Did* she, Madame?"

"I could not tell," she muttered. "I had already covered the Madonna with two layers of a protective substance."

"But you warned Van Dam."

She did not answer, then desperately she burst out with:

"I did not know what he would do. You must understand. I never dreamt he was capable of it. Tsuda's death was an accident. André did not mean to kill him."

"I am not concerned with intentions! Van Dam may have intended this, or that." The *commissario* was ironical. "He caused Tsuda's death."

"It was not murder," protested Juliette. "Tsuda was suspicious. He refused to give André a lift. André had to use force. And when he hit him, Tsuda . . . just died."

"Yes, yes, yes. He just died." Gadda's lips sketched an unpleasant smile. Then he said viciously, "Did you tell Van Dam that Doris Boot saw you working over the painting?"

"I told him," whispered Juliette. "I told André she must have seen what I was doing in my room. Because last night, by the fire, she was talking to Professor Mowbray and she said she had seen two Madonnas. She seemed to be trying to tell him where the Bellini was—or to warn me that she knew what I had done.

"Then, later Doris told me that she went into André's room Saturday night and found it empty. She asked me if she should tell *you.*"

"And you told Van Dam?" asked Gadda sternly.

Juliette assented. She began to sob.

"Just so," snapped the *commissario.* "She was full of information, Doris Boot, which she had only to fit together—which she had perhaps already fitted together. She was dangerous."

The *commissario* turned, and at a mere flicker of his eyelid, two policemen moved in, one on each side of the Dutchman.

XXIV

"Let us turn to the death of Raffaella Mowbray." The *commissario* was being almost schoolmasterish, but no class-room had ever suffered such tension. "Why was she killed? Because of the Madonna? When Raffaella Mowbray died she no longer had her. Van Dam's plan to get the Madonna was simple and should have succeeded. In any case he and Juliette were out here talking until two o'clock in the morning."

Gadda's eyes moved from face to face.

"Raffaella Mowbray was last seen at about ten minutes to ten and she died before midnight. The medical evidence is conclusive.

"She is at the centre of all this. A young woman of considerable attractions. She has grown up in very modest circumstances in the north of Italy. At an early age, she falls in love, but she does not wish to marry the young man. There is no money. In the Italy of towards fifteen years ago it is unwise. They part, he to go to Milan, she to come to Rome."

The *commissario* broke off suddenly and walked behind the audience to the projector, which he plugged in. At a sign from him, Augusto hurried to close the outer door and to draw curtains across both windows. On the screen the Madonna gradually emerged from a country background, her beautiful face framed by the folds of a pale robe, clasping the Child in her arms. A ripple of excitement passed over the figures seated before her.

"You get the full force of the painting on the screen," said the *commissario*. "Probably hard to hang anything much more appealing than that on your wall at home. I wonder if any of you have noticed something about her . . ."

Swinging around, he surveyed them once more.

"Well, of course," Jo Ann spoke without thinking, "she's rather like . . ."

"She is very like Raffaella." Renato's lips trembled. "The features, and the sweetness and gravity of the expression. The skin too—full of shades, even a hint of green. A lovely, lovely skin . . ."

Grotesquely, with awful comic effect, his voice rose in a squeak and he burst into sobs.

"Yes, the painting is like the Signora Mowbray." The *commissario* cut Renato short, perhaps in impatience, perhaps in compassion. "Quite remarkably like, in fact. Well, to resume. She came to Rome. In Rome she trained as a secretary and studied languages. It was a hard life, until she got a job with the banking Consortium. Soon after, she met—and married—a man who is famous, a man wholly wrapped up in the world of art, a man many years her senior. Why did she marry him? She was so much younger than he was. She no doubt felt it necessary to marry. She wanted security . . ."

The *commissario*, who was facing the screen, now glowing with colour and light, and who was talking deliberately and tellingly—so he thought—was startled by the touch of a hand on his shoulder. He swung round to look up into the face of Charles Mowbray.

"You must not tell her story, Commissario. It is not yours to tell, and you will do it so ill." Mowbray's face was sardonic, even if ash white; his eyes beautiful and compelling, even if tragedy was in their depths; his tall figure so carelessly aristocratic beside the lumpy form of the *commissario*.

"She married me, Commissario, because—as you say—she had no prospects and because, in a country where the entrancing, mobile faces beloved of fifteenth-century artists still crowd the streets, the singular beauty of a Bellini Madonna will not necessarily remark attention. It is no pretty-pretty kind of beauty and has no vulgar appeal. Her beauty was of a severe and reserved character, depending on delicacy of line and a haunting, brooding quality of expression, on a skin capable of a thousand different transmutations of colour made on it by the reflection of light and shade. She had a skin the like of which I've never seen—as white as a lily, which the green of the grass, the blue of the sky tinged with a hue hardly describable. There were the shades of winter, and the shades of summer, the reflections of the subdued light of indoors, and the challenging brilliance of the noonday sun. And her skin responded marvellously to them all.

"She married me, Commissario, because in me she found an instinctive perception and appreciation of her plastic qualities, a fit setting for them. She was irresistibly drawn to me. She could do nothing else. For three years she was ideally happy with me and my life was little short of perfect."

Mowbray paused, gazing at the screen, lost in thought, and there was scarcely a breath to break the stillness. Then he swung round once more to face his persecutor.

"It was fated to end. I was growing old. Work pressed. Money was short. My work was absorbing, hers a continuous trial. She made good money, but she was not at home in the high-powered tempo of an organisation such as the Consortium. How could it be otherwise? Her forte was to be a woman, her special capacity including a vast reserve of wisdom, understanding, tenderness. How could she be anything else, with that face? No marriage is devoid of strain. If the life of the office left her feeling inadequate, the lives of those who made it up incited in her, I think, a desire for excitement, adventure, money, travel, none of which she enjoyed with me. She . . . We grew apart."

"She wanted . . . she wanted a child!" Barbicinti's voice broke in, violent and shaken. "A Madonna! You saw her always as a Madonna. But is the Madonna ever without the Child? You put her in a frame, on a pedestal. She wanted life, not an idyll . . . It was too exacting, the life of a Madonna . . ."

Mowbray winced, as at a whiplash, and fell silent, motionless, his eyes terrible.

The *commissario*'s gaze faltered, then flickered away from that tortured face. As Mowbray made no attempt to continue, Gadda himself took up the tale, in quiet but emphatic tones.

"Perhaps, Dr. Mowbray, it was the feeling that you might one day lose your wife that caused you to take out insurance in the form of the Bellini painting. Whatever the reason, the fact that this stolen work of art was hanging in your apartment must, I think, have produced a revulsion of feeling for you in your wife.

She must have been worried, perhaps frightened. She must have known how intrinsically bound up with her own person was this stolen masterpiece. She must have felt partially responsible for it. And it must also have been a continual reminder to her of how you regarded her . . ."

"More than anything, it drained us of money." Mowbray's voice was scarcely audible, his head bowed. "I had no part in its theft; when the Madonna came my way, however, I could not resist the temptation to acquire her. I succumbed; and it took all my savings to buy her. Raffaella began to hate me for it . . ."

"Probably," said the *commissario* carefully, "Mr. John Backhouse offered an escape from a situation which grew more and more oppressive for her. It was inevitable that any man of sensitivity who was thrown into close contact with her should feel her influence. She worked for him for five years, and it was of small importance to him that she was not highly efficient. He fell in love with her. And she—with him? He had, at any rate, attraction for her."

There was a short bark of laughter from John Backhouse, inevitably followed by that characteristic clearing of the throat.

"You have something to add?" asked Gadda.

"I have nothing to add, to your masterly exposition." A dark red slowly crept up Backhouse's face and he spoke compulsively, the words wrenched from him. "I am glad to know that she felt at least some attraction for the man she intended to marry."

"Let me continue, Mr. Backhouse," said the *commissario* smoothly, feeling very much as though he were walking a tightrope. "The attachment between the two of you did not go unnoticed in the close-knit office setting. Your wife found out. Then, with the exigencies of work in the Consortium, Signora Mowbray was no longer needed. In your absence she was dismissed.

"For you, Mr. Backhouse, it was the turning-point. Her dismissal was going to leave an emptiness, a gap which was insupportable. You felt you could not face life without her, and decided to ask your wife for a divorce. When Raffaella Mowbray told her husband she was leaving him, he asked her to wait, not to rush into it, to stop seeing Backhouse for some months. And she agreed. Dr. Mowbray had now come to a point in his life which he might have felt was inevitable, but was not the easier to bear for that."

The *commissario* kept his eyes on the floor now, raising them only to glance briefly, in the semi-darkness, at his victims. He singled out Beverley now.

"Mrs. Backhouse—what did Mrs. Backhouse feel? She was to lose husband, home, residence in a city she has known all her life, friends—one friend in particular. Mrs. Backhouse became very jealous, and she began to hate. It was more than Hedda Hardegen could bear to see. Hedda had already written an anonymous letter to Dr. Mowbray. She wondered if more drastic measures were necessary."

The *commissario* paused. His listeners were utterly still, sitting there in the half-darkness.

"On top of all this," he went on, "Signor Barbicinti turns up again in Rome. In Raffaella, old passions, long dormant, revive with force. Since her marriage to Professor Mowbray, moreover, she has come once more to reduced circumstances. And whenever she enters the study, the Madonna, who is the cause of it, looks down on her. She decides to sell the Bellini Madonna for half a million dollars and to run off with Barbicinti on the proceeds. At one stroke she will have her revenge on the Madonna who has cost her so much, gain the man she has never ceased to love, and provide them both with enough money to live comfortably.

"She brings the Madonna up here to sell it to Mr. Tsuda, the Japanese millionaire.

"On Saturday morning, John Backhouse arrives back from abroad. By chance, he finds in his wife's bedroom a photograph of Raffaella which has served as a target for her revolver practice and is riddled with bullet holes. He checks to see if his wife has her gun with her, and not finding it, he jumps in his car and follows. He is not to know that the previous afternoon Raffaella's car has come to grief on the way. Someone tampered with it."

Gadda's eyes were riveted on Hedda, for all to see. He was silent for a full moment.

"Of course, the person concerned denies it and it will probably never be proved."

Someone uttered a little, hopeless exclamation. The *commissario* was conscious of Hedda and Beverley clinging together, of Backhouse's stony expression. Satisfied that his point had been taken, he continued.

"Up here in the monastery, the group settles in. Dr. Mowbray is anxious to provide an atmosphere, a particular background for his lecture. The frescoes are inspected, he gives a talk on the Benedictines. The weather, which has turned stormy, adds drama. Before dinner on Saturday night there is a move to the cells. In Mrs. Partridge's cell drinks are served about six-thirty to seven. Where was Raffaella Mowbray then?"

"Before dinner," Barbicinti's voice broke in, "she and I were together out on the terrace."

"Quite so," agreed the *commissario*. "And to gain the big hall, Mr. Backhouse would certainly have had to cross the terrace." He did not bother to elaborate further.

"Between six-thirty and seven, Beverley Backhouse and Hedda are doing what? We do not know. But at some stage Hedda took Beverley's gun from her handbag and hid it on the window-ledge outside in the corridor. She says she did it for safety's sake. Beverley Backhouse, at least, could not see it there.

"Dinner follows, and immediately afterwards John Backhouse arrives. He goes off to change his wet clothes. Coffee is served and towards eight o'clock everyone leaves the hall for the cells. Only Dr. Mowbray and his wife remain here to prepare for the lecture.

"At about ten past eight Mrs. Boot returns to the kitchen for drinking water. She overhears a quarrel between the Mowbrays. After they move away, she goes to the kitchen for her water. She listens to *Canzonissima* for a while. It is being relayed on Augusto's transistor. Augusto, by the way, tells me he quite inadvertently allowed the sound of the radio to be relayed to the cells. He says he placed it in the ante-room and turned it up when *Canzonissima* began because it is a large transistor and he did not want to risk getting it wet while he and his wife were washing up the dishes.

"Mrs. Boot went back to the cells about eight-thirty-five or so. Augusto moved the transistor to the kitchen again a few minutes before nine o'clock and the noise was cut off in the cells.

"Now, at about eight-forty or a minute or two after, Dr. Mowbray and his wife walked back together to their respective cells. Signor Barbicinti, who made several attempts to find Signora Mowbray between eight-forty and her return to this hall at nine-twenty-five, saw no sign of her."

The *commissario* turned to Augusto once more and enquired, in Italian, if the man had seen her during that period. Augusto shook his head.

"Where was she during this time, if not in her cell?" asked Gadda. "Did any of you see her?"

There was no response to his question.

"At nine-twenty-five, when Dr. Mowbray knocked on her door, she was back in her cell, because she answered him, and shortly afterwards followed him out here. Now during this period after dinner, and until nine-twenty-five, when the bell sounded for the lecture, you were all in your cells. Right? All except for Mr. Backhouse, who returned to his cell some time after nine o'clock. He cannot remember exactly when.

"Lady Loftus, you can probably speak for the ladies. All were in the sleeping quarters?"

"We were all in Mrs. Partridge's cell for a little." Lady Loftus's voice lacked volume and positively trembled.

"You heard *Canzonissima?*"

"Yes, it startled all of us," put in Jo Ann. "Everyone checked to see if it could be heard in their own rooms."

"You can confirm that it finished at a few minutes to nine?"

"About then. I remember thinking we had been spared a good deal of it."

"Did anyone *not* hear it in the cells?" The *commissario*'s eyes roved round. "That is, except for Mr. Backhouse, who was still out here at the time?" No one said a word, so he continued.

"You are quite sure, Dr. Mowbray, that when you and your wife returned to your cells at eight-forty approximately, this music was still coming through?"

Mowbray, who had slumped in his chair, started and stared at Gadda.

"Oh yes, it went on for a good fifteen minutes, I should think. Dreadful noise. I had stretched out on my bed. I wanted to rest before the lecture, but with that unearthly row going on I couldn't collect my thoughts. I was just about to get up and go out to tell Augusto to turn it off, as I guessed what had happened. But then it suddenly ceased."

"So, we can at least be quite sure that Signora Mowbray was in her cell at eight-forty-five." The *commissario*'s eyes played endlessly over their faces. "We come now to the lecture. Signor Barbicinti, you all came in, a little before nine-thirty, in a group, except for Mr. Backhouse and Mrs. Boot. The hall was in darkness, the first slide already illuminated. I am right?"

"Yes."

"Signora Mowbray—where was she when you arrived?"

"Sitting by the projector at the back of the audience."

"Did anyone speak to her?"

"Naturally not." It was Barbicinti again. "Dr. Mowbray began his lecture almost at once."

"Standing in this position?" The *commissario* indicated Mowbray's chair, right at the back of the audience.

There was a murmur of assent from them all.

"And the Signora Mowbray was sitting at the projector. Behind you. And at a little before ten o'clock she went out, to her death. The only possible suspects are Mr. Backhouse, Mrs. Backhouse, or Mrs. Hardegen."

From being almost casual, the *commissario* became angry.

"One of you is lying," he rapped out. "Either you, Mr. Backhouse, or you, Mrs. Backhouse, or you, Mrs. Hardegen. Because, if each of you is telling the truth, we must look elsewhere for the killer. But the rest of you were present at the lecture. If one of you is responsible, then the Signora Mowbray was killed not during but before the lecture. But she herself was present, until ten to ten. You all say so, every one of you. On this there is general agreement."

The *commissario* paused; then his voice dropped as he continued quietly but very clearly.

"But did you in fact see her? The hall was in darkness on your entry, the whole of your attention concentrated on the screen from the very first moment. I put it to you, all of you, that you did not in fact see the Signora Mowbray. I put it to you that because she had always worked the slide machine during Dr. Mowbray's lectures, you simply assumed her presence. There was nothing to deny it. And you heard her go out. But did you? You heard the door open and shut, but did you see her?"

Gadda paused once more. The silence was awful. Covert glances were sent towards Mowbray, but now Mowbray was leaning back almost indolently in his chair, with an impassive expression.

"Professor Mowbray has told us that he opened the door himself for his wife and that he talked to her briefly. She whispered that she felt unwell and needed to leave the lecture. But for this we have only Professor Mowbray's word." The *commissario*'s voice shook slightly, and a flush crept up over his face, usually so pale. "Who saw her?" he demanded of them.

"Why, one can't swear to having seen her, it's true," Lady Loftus said fearfully. "It was so dark when we came in, and that was the only chance we would have had. Once seated, we couldn't have seen her without standing up and turning right round."

"Can anyone *swear* to having seen her?"

"We were not thinking of her, for one thing, I guess." It was Jo Ann. "We didn't have time, with the lecture beginning as soon as we shuffled into place. I would have said I heard the Mowbrays whispering together, though, when Raffaella went out."

"Whispers can be deceptive."

"It is true her presence could have been simulated." There was wildness in Barbicinti's voice.

In silence, the *commissario*'s eyes searched the frightened faces before him. No one moved or spoke, and the *commissario* slowly shifted his gaze to meet Mowbray's ironic glance.

"You maintain, Dr. Mowbray, that your wife was present, during the early part of the lecture?"

"Can you prove she wasn't?" asked Mowbray, almost conversationally.

As he answered, the *commissario*'s voice was a little loud and out of control. But his dumpy figure seemed to grow in stature at the same time. "I can prove that at eight-forty you did not hear the music of *Canzonissima* in your cell."

Mowbray's expression did not change.

"How is that, Commissario?"

"Because, Doctor, your cell—the end one, as well as the one next door to it, which was uninhabited—does not share in the peculiar acoustic properties of the others. A fact which you had, apparently, never checked. You did not drop off to sleep just now, for instance, when Augusto rang the bell. You simply did not hear it."

Gadda was nervous to desperation. It made him adopt a hectoring tone. But Mowbray's response was surprising. His hand came down with a slap on the arm of his chair and he exclaimed:

"*Per Bacco!* You're right. I never checked it. I never even thought of that possibility!"

Gadda, caught off balance, was suddenly furious.

"Don't adopt that tone with me, sir!"

Mowbray got to his feet with an impatient gesture, as if to dismiss such nonsense.

"But of course it does not constitute proof of my being guilty of murder, Commissario! You do realise that!"

"Why else would you lie so deliberately about your movements at that critical time?" demanded Gadda angrily.

"Wait a bit, Commissario." Mowbray was fencing, taking desperate risks, but keeping his head magnificently. "Suppose I said I was deaf, but was loath to admit it—that the reason I lied about hearing *Canzonissima* was because, quite simply, I was sensitive on the point? Old people, as you know, often won't admit their failing powers."

"So," Gadda gritted his teeth. "Now you maintain you are deaf."

"I said, suppose I had maintained it! I'm simply pointing out that my lie could have been a comparatively innocent one, and that you could not have *proved* it otherwise!"

"I would be grateful," said Gadda threateningly, "if you would stick to facts."

"Commissario," replied Mowbray, with perfect self-possession. "I am conceited enough to want to establish that you are able to make no case against me—for lack of proof. That is all."

"You're saying now that—"

Mowbray held up a hand. For a little, he was the teacher

again, encouraging a bright pupil. He said, almost soothingly, "You have sorted out this awful tangle so well, Commissario. Let me say, at this point, that I am not deaf and I did lie about hearing *Canzonissima.*"

Gadda burst out savagely: "Which can mean only one thing!"

"It is not my habit to lie," said Mowbray disdainfully. "You see, even though my wife met her death at my hand—"

"Ah!" Gadda couldn't let him finish, and his triumphant exclamation sounded across the hall like a clarion call.

XXV

"You had already killed her when you went back to your cell!"

The *commissario* was breathing hard, with a cold glitter in his eyes. Mowbray had infuriated him, but he had now regained control of himself, and swiftly the roles of the two men were once more reversed. The *commissario* was an instrument of justice now, utterly intent.

"From the moment you pocketed the gun, everything played into your hands. Mrs. Backhouse's wild talk at dinner, Backhouse's arrival. You took your wife out on the terrace when you believed everyone was safely out of the way. The shot would easily pass for an electrical report even if anyone were to hear it. With luck, the body would not be discovered till morning. You had planned a perfect alibi.

"You shot her and went back to your cell. At ten minutes to ten, in the darkness, you staged your wife's exit from the lecture. Whoever was to be suspected of this murder, it could not be you. You were careful, after the lecture, to remain in the hall for hours more. You put up a most marvellous performance, too.

"Things turned out better for you still. Mrs. Backhouse left the lecture soon after Raffaella's faked departure, and then Mrs. Hardegen as well."

A shriek startled the *commissario* and he swung round as Juliette rose and tottered towards Mowbray. Her face was horror-stricken.

"Not here—not now! Not before all!" she stammered. "Not

now, the end . . ." Sinking into a chair, she covered her face with her hands, her shoulders heaving.

Unexpectedly, the *commissario* found himself obeying her.

"Clear the hall and leave us," he said to Dante.

Escorted by the police officers, the others slowly filed out and the heavy door closed behind them. Gadda, Juliette and Mowbray were left alone. And Mowbray suddenly slumped.

"I misjudged you, Commissario." Mowbray, very white, lay back in his chair and his words came with difficulty. "You are almost right. But you ascribe to me a cold-blooded devilishness of design and execution that is not justified. You must believe me that when I came up here I had not the slightest intention, nor ever had, of killing my wife."

"You can say that *now* . . ."

"No, Commissario, no intention in the world. When I . . . shot my wife," Mowbray's face quivered, "she had made me feel such revulsion that my hand functioned almost independently of my brain. I shot a devil I hadn't known existed."

"Why, then—"

"The Raffaella I had known was no more." Mowbray's eyes were unfocused. He was silent for a moment before he said: "The Bellini Madonna began a chain of events that ended in disaster. As you discovered, to buy it took most of our savings. Yes, madness if you like, Commissario. You could never understand it. Madness, also, to Raffaella when I finally told her. She blamed me bitterly. She had been poor before. She had worked hard. She feared poverty again."

"But she was leaving you. You had agreed to it."

"Ah, to marry Backhouse, yes." Mowbray looked absently at the *commissario*. "But I had a hope that she would give him up, you see."

"Then Barbicinti turned up."

"Renato Barbicinti turned up. He came back and he possessed her. Perhaps you can in some measure understand the feelings of a man who sees his wife . . ." Mowbray's face darkened, and his voice was suddenly rough, not his own. "When I tried to speak to her . . . she had turned into someone else. She told me her life was at last her own. To be free of me there was nothing she was not capable of. And then she said something that made me suspicious. Finally I dragged it out of her. And she told me, out there on the terrace, that she had sold my Madonna."

For a moment the eyes dulled and the jaw sagged. Something or someone quite unfamiliar was before them, before the face they knew as Mowbray's re-formed.

"I did not even understand she had brought the Madonna up here, nor did I suspect Tsuda. I'd never met Tsuda before and I had not connected him with the man who made the original offer for the Madonna.

"But in one stroke, Raffaella took everything from me I held most dear. There was a madness, a wildness, a force in her I'd never seen. My Raffaella, my sweet and grave and gentle Raffaella—talking ruthlessly and wantonly, telling me things . . . things a man should never hear of himself. She took from me everything she had ever given me."

"She had come down from her frame." The *commissario* hardly noticed that he had spoken.

"She had come down from her frame," Mowbray repeated. "I had to get rid of that Raffaella. I made to grab her by the throat. I would have strangled her then. And she pulled a gun from her pocket."

"*She* had the gun! You are trying to pretend—"

"I am trying to pretend nothing. She certainly got the gun from the ledge. I saw it myself before dinner; I even mentioned it to her. I understand now that she was scared of Beverley Backhouse. Or of someone. Whoever had tampered with her car. It had nearly caused her death. She knew very little of guns. I easily got it from her. And I shot her." Mowbray's eyes were suddenly veiled again. "Her body went over with the impact." His hands clenched, and sweat beaded his forehead. "Afterwards, I went back to my room. And as I went down the corridor, I heard, through an open door, Mrs. Boot giving her version, with the utmost enjoyment, of the passage between Raffaella and myself in the big hall. I knew my guilt would be immediately apparent.

"Inside my room I tried to pull myself together. I felt it wrong I should be accused of murder. The rest you know . . ."

Mowbray, calm now, his face relaxed, looked like a man resting after great exertions. His eyes went to Juliette's tear-stained face and he remarked:

"You won't get your course of lectures, I'm afraid."

She raised her eyes to his and her lips formed words which she could not utter.

"Both of us wanted the Madonna, Juliette. You for money, I for love. At least we each of us knew her quality." He smiled at her.

It broke Juliette's scant control immediately. She burst into a storm of frantic tears.

The *commissario*, gesturing to Dante, walked slowly from the hall. He felt exhausted, drained of all feeling.

Curtain

The road was open, though care would be needed. The foreman of the road-gang had given the word. On the Wednesday morning, the little party—so depleted now—quickly made preparations for departure, with hardly any talk. One by one they bade Lucia and Augusto farewell. In silence, the Italian couple stood at the top of the staircase watching them make their way down to the lower level.

John Backhouse had a protective arm around Beverley's shoulders, another around Hedda's, and his face, at least, seemed turned resolutely to the future. Only Jo Ann Partridge talked, once clear of the steps, and then in a voice lower than usual, to Louise Parsons. It would be a little while before the women were in full voice again.

"A terrible business, Louise. Lucia said there was a curse on the place, and I wouldn't say she was wrong."

"Well, you do feel fate played a part in this chain of accidents. All for the Madonna," Louise said disbelievingly.

"To think the Madonna will go back to a corner of the Galleria Borghese and brood away there, after the tragedy she's caused!" mused Jo Ann.

After a moment's silence Louise said abruptly:

"Mowbray and Van Dam . . . What a world of difference between them. Mowbray stole, and killed, for love. While Van Dam was impelled by greed."

"Van Dam—if you believe him—didn't mean to kill Tsuda. But Doris . . . Oh God," Jo Ann shuddered. "A cold-blooded, criminal act."

"Mowbray was mad, mad at the thought his wife had turned against him."

"Ah, Raffaella had the misfortune to fail to measure up to a man's idea of her," returned Jo Ann solemnly.

"Oh, it was awful, at the end, to hear Mowbray talking of her," Louise said huskily.

"Yes, it was. He was trying to recreate the image of the woman he had married, the one whose character matched her face."

"Having destroyed the real woman," put in Louise.

"Mowbray should have been married to Juliette," Jo Ann suddenly said.

"You're right. She's not only an artist, but she had a high regard for Mowbray. You could tell when she looked at him and talked about him. That was genuine. She was, of course, also prepared to steal."

"Well, what Juliette has done she'll pay for," grimaced Jo Ann.

"Renato Barbicinti is in an awful state." Louise's eyes were on the tragic figure of the young man, who strode on alone, head down.

"We all are," said Jo Ann grimly. "We're all at the end of our tether."

"The final act was the worst of all, to me," faltered Louise.

"It's a wonder to me the *commissario* let Mowbray go down to the frescoes for all that time." Jo Ann shook her head.

"It was Mowbray's last request, to be allowed to spend an hour alone with the frescoes. Perhaps Italians *are* more human sometimes, even policemen." Louise shivered.

"How could the *commissario* have forgotten the sheer drop from the outside porch down there?"

"You don't think it occurred to the *commissario* that Mowbray . . ."

"No, I don't," returned Jo Ann decisively. "No policeman in his senses would want to take the rap for that."

"So much died with Mowbray." Louise was near to tears. "All his knowledge, all his high ideals . . ."

"And all his misconceptions about his wife."

"Don't talk about it." Louise's voice rose hysterically. "It's over now. I want to get away—and forget."

With a burst of golden light, the sun emerged brilliantly from behind gathering clouds, gilding the grave faces of the men and women who walked away down the road and outlining the helicopter of the *Carabinieri.*

And so peace returned to the lonely, lovely place of Saint Benedict.